# Extreme Edge

# Extreme Edge

Heather Kellerhals-Stewart

James Lorimer & Company Ltd., Publishers
Toronto

James Lorimer & Company Ltd. acknowledges the support of the Ontario Arts Council. We acknowledge the support of the Government of Canada through the Book Publishing Industry Development Program (BPIDP) for our publishing activities. We acknowledge the support of the Canada Council for the Arts for our publishing program. We acknowledge the support of the Government of Ontario through the Ontario Media Development Corporation's Ontario Book Initiative.

Cover design: Clarke MacDonald

**Library and Archives Canada Cataloguing in Publication**

Kellerhals-Stewart, Heather, 1937-
    Extreme edge / Heather Kellerhals-Stewart.

(SideStreets)
ISBN 978-1-55028-967-1(bound)—978-1-55028-966-4 (pbk.)

I. Title. II. Series

PS8571.E447E98 2007      jC813'.54      C2007-900356-7

James Lorimer & Company Ltd.,
Publishers
317 Adelaide Street West
Suite 1002
Toronto, Ontario
M5V 1P9
www.lorimer.ca

Distributed in the
U.S. by:
Orca Book Publishers
P.O. Box 468
Custer, WA USA
98240-0468

Printed and bound in Canada

*For Cecile McGoran and
our good times in the mountains*

# Acknowledgements

Thanks to climbers Rolf Kellerhals,
Erika Kellerhals, Markus Kellerhals and
Tanya Binette for reading the text and for sharing
their amazing knowledge of the climbing world,
even down to the latest jargon.
Thanks also to Dorothy Whittington, who
worked for many years with the Quadra
ambulance service, for her help and suggestions.
Children's book editor, Hadley Dyer, kept me on
track with her sense of humour and patience.

# Chapter 1

I do not like ice climbing. The freezing air makes my eyes water and catches in my throat. Each painful breath rises in a small puff. So what am I doing hanging off this frozen waterfall? I could be skiing or rock climbing, even hanging out at the mall. Anywhere else would do. I look over my shoulder and see cars snaking along the highway far below. The restaurant is a pinprick beside the road. They'll be serving up the usual lukewarm coffee, hamburgers, greasy fries and I can just taste that hot chocolate with whipped cream sliding across my tongue.

From where I'm standing on this precarious ice knob I can see the brown smudge of the city, and the ocean sparkling like a million candles. Why can't my climbing partner keep moving? My feet are freezing inside these plastic boots. I wiggle my dead toes around, then kick my crampon's front points more securely into the blue ice.

"Brad!" I finally call. "What's the problem up there?"

The rope between me and my climbing partner vibrates. "I've hit the crux, Jay. It'll be tough pulling myself over the ice bulge here."

"Yeah?" Looking up I see what he means. The bulge is where the frozen water plunges over a rock outcrop. Ice is thinner there too. He's struggling, with both legs splayed out and arms overhead, gripping his two ice picks. "Have you got a decent ice screw in there?"

"Hope so. It feels bomber."

I check my own belay point — two ice screws placed a half metre apart in the thick ice and connected to my harness by a sling. Solid for now, but if the temperature keeps rising we could be in trouble.

"Hurry up, Brad."

"Give me half a second, okay? I'm trying to squeeze in another screw."

"Sure, Brad ... sorry. Do whatever you have to." Relax, I tell myself. You know Brad has been having a tough time trying to keep up with guys like the Iceman over there.

I lean back on my belay watching the other rope party climbing above us. We're not in their direct line of fire. The Iceman, who is leading, moves like a cougar stalking its prey. He follows a projecting ice tongue, then exits onto a rock platform near the top, as far as anyone can safely go today.

Beyond that the ice gets too thin. Within minutes he is belaying his partner up and the two of them are out of the game. No messing around for the Iceman. Why do you think he got his name?

"Move, Brad," I say under my breath.

I take a deep breath to relax. The cold air is freezing my nose, and it has found its way through my gloves and into my fingers. To make things worse, ice shards slither down the frozen surface and explode in my face.

"Damned ice screw," Brad says. "The ice is too chandeliered. I almost lost the screw."

Sure, on my head, I think.

A crowd has gathered in the parking lot below, watching us like a pack of dogs sniffing out trouble. I look away, trying to escape this frozen world around me. White haze is blurring the horizon and hiding the distant islands. The sky is still a deep blue overhead, but I'm feeling a change in the air.

"Brad, we need to bail. I think a weather system is moving in. How's it looking up there?"

"I'm trying to find a decent screw placement."

"Why not come down? We can exit somewhere below me."

"It's probably quicker to keep heading up."

"Listen, Brad, we don't have time to mess around with screws." I slip off one glove and draw a finger across the frozen waterfall surface. "It's starting to soften."

"I know ... You think I don't know? I'm trying to hurry."

My throat feels dry as I suck in air. Neither of us are experienced ice climbers. Why did I let myself get talked into coming? Because I'm Brad's friend and we've done hundreds of climbs together and no one else would partner with him today. Idiot! You should stick with what you know — rock, not ice.

"Brad!" I shout.

No reply. A chunk of ice wings past me. Small maybe, but a warning of what might come. The whole glazing on the rock outcrop above us could break loose. And Brad with it, if he doesn't move. Yes ... the air is definitely getting warmer and the white haze I saw before is creeping claw-like over the sky.

"Brad, are you okay?"

All I can hear are his crampons scraping the surface. Ice particles are showering over me. If it wasn't for the helmet I'm wearing, my hair would be white. I think it's turning white anyway.

Finally Brad's voice echoes down. "I gotta rest. Figure out my next move."

Oh great, so what do we do now? I look up and see the Iceman's head peering over the crest of the frozen waterfall. "You two should be off there. The air temperature is rising. That whole thing is starting to drip. I can hear water gurgling under the ice."

"Yeah, like my sick stomach," I mutter.

"Forget the pro'," he tells Brad. "You'll never find a decent screw placement there. How be I toss down a line and a couple of ascenders so you can jug your way up and out?"

As usual the Iceman is full of climbing jargon.

"Why not?" Brad calls back, trying to sound cool.

"I'd belay you up myself," the Iceman says, "but I'm out of here. Too much stuff coming down. It's not healthy."

The Iceman moves back from the edge. I watch him attaching some slings and ascenders to his rope, then lowering it to where Brad is hanging like some helpless beetle.

Trouble is, I'm feeling pretty helpless too. The Iceman is right, it's not healthy here. How long is this exercise going to take?

"I've tied your rope into our usual belay tree here," the Iceman calls down. "It's bomber."

I watch Brad messing around with the climbing hardware. He fumbles, almost dropping one ascender. Retrieves it at the last moment, clasps it in a bear hug and leans back against the ice. I can hear his heavy breathing.

"Come on, Brad, you can do it."

"For sure. Hang in there, Jay. It'll be your turn soon."

He seems to take forever. I watch him clamping the ascenders onto the rope. Up one step, move the ascender higher. Another step. Slide the ascender up. Clamp it onto the rope again. Same thing over and over. Great ... he's finally made it over the ice bulge. I hear his crampons scraping on bare rock.

Brad pulls up the slack in our rope. "You want me to bring you up, Jay?"

"How's it look, have you got a decent belay?"

"Nothing bombproof."

"Then get yourself up and out. My ice screws here are solid."

"Okay, whatever you say." A second later his head reappears. "You sure? I don't like leaving you on your own."

"Yes, I'm positive. Just go ... go."

Is it fear or cold cramping my leg muscles? You should never have let the Iceman talk you into this, Brad. My gloves are wet now and I take turns shaking my freezing hands. If the knob I'm standing on was more substantial I'd feel a lot better.

I make the mistake of glancing down. The crowd in the parking lot below has expanded. More cars are turning in and people are milling around. I can see their upturned faces.

"What are you idiots waiting for?" I grumble. I'm angry with myself ... with everybody. Angry with Brad for dragging me here. Angry with the Iceman for having to rescue us. Look, I'm the sixteen-year-old rock rat who climbs by himself with no rope or aid. And it doesn't feel good having to be rescued.

Whang! A small chunk of ice bounces off my left ice pick. Although it doesn't dislodge the pick, the sound gives me a start. Smaller particles slither after it with the same sound as waves washing against a shoreline. White haze has now camou-flaged the sun. Somewhere water is dripping.

I hear Brad calling. "Jay, I've made it. Half a second and I'll belay you up."

"Whatever you do, make it quick, Brad."

"Okay, you're on belay."

Sweet, words those. They slide down like chocolate on the tongue. "Climbing," I call back.

When I reach over to remove the two ice crews, one pulls out without even turning, the other isn't much better. I shake my head and lean my chest against the frozen waterfall. My whole body starts shaking.

"You coming, Jay?"

"Yeah, coming."

I dislodge one ice pick, reach overhead and swing it into the ice. I move the other pick up, swing it. Both my arms are overhead. I move so fast Brad has problems keeping my rope tight. I cruise over the ice bulge that gave him all that trouble.

As I stop on the platform to catch my breath, Brad looks down, a big grin creasing his face. "Whew, I can breathe easier seeing you over the crux."

Another ice chunk wings its way past me. "Yeah, Brad and I'll breathe easier when we're both standing on bare ground." But there is genuine concern in both our voices, I can see it in Brad's face.

Climbing has started my blood circulating

again. I hear myself crying out as heat explodes into my hands and feet. "Aaah ..."

Brad's head nods in sympathy. "Frozen feet coming back to life, right?"

"That's one way of putting it."

I'm just swinging my left ice pick, maybe three metres above the ice bulge now and thinking I'm home free when Brad yells, "Ice fall!"

I look up in time to see a huge ice chunk hurtle past my shoulder and go crashing onto the platform where I was standing a few seconds ago. It shatters into a thousand pieces. The *ooh* that floats up from the crowd below drowns my own gasp.

"Jay ... you all right?"

"Uh ... I guess."

For the next few minutes I forget any climbing style. My aim is to get out — fast. I use the rope to ease my way up. Brad is keeping it tight. As I'm nearing the top, I can actually see water seeping across the ice. I'm soaked. And everything hurts.

Brad reaches a hand over the edge and helps me up. "Way to go, Jay."

We retrieve the Iceman's rope from the belay tree, and then we're off the ice and onto the trail. We sit there silently, watching the scene below. "I bet some of those bums down there are disappointed we didn't crater," Brad finally says.

"It was a pretty close call. You won't get me ice climbing again soon."

"Yeah, I won't let the Iceman talk me into another crazy operation."

The southeast wind is drawing in warmer air, licking away at the ice. Yes, it's a good time to be off. I give Brad a shove. "There's food waiting below. What will it be, Brad?"

"A side of fries, with lots of ketchup."

"So let's go."

# Chapter 2

After drying out in the restaurant, Brad and I pile into his old pickup truck and head for town. It'll take us a good half hour. I settle into the passenger seat, but don't make myself too comfortable. I want to stay alert. We're both tired after the early morning start and the hours spent on the frozen waterfall. It's too easy to fall asleep. For a while I actually do manage to keep a watchful eye on the road ...

The sound of Brad swearing and the squeal of brakes brings me back to life. "Crazy driver! Cut right in front of me. Almost caused an accident."

I kick myself for dozing off. To make sure Brad stays awake I keep talking. "Another week and we'll be into March. Are you going to keep working weekends at Whistler until the end of the ski season?"

"It keeps bread on the table," he reminds me.

"And I don't mind working at the beginner's lift. The kids are funny the way they fall down, get up ... like they're made of rubber. They appreciate my rotten jokes too."

Brad smiles as he talks about kids learning to ski. That's what I like about him — he's a genuinely kind character. And he's a fun climbing partner, if you keep him off ice.

"I've also got a part-time job at the Pizza Palace," Brad goes on. "Pay is minimum wage, but it helps. I get by okay."

"Sure." I nod my head, amazed again at how different our lives are. Brad has no family to speak of — his parents split up last year, mother is in the States now, father working in northern Alberta, a half brother living somewhere else. And me? My family bugs me sometimes, but I do have one. Plus there's Katy — my friend and "climbing buddy," as she calls me. Our family can even talk together, at least until dad starts arguing and thumping his fist on the table. That's when my mom and sister decide they have to go pee, sticking me with the lecture. Thinking about my weird family gets me laughing.

"What's so funny, Jay?"

"Oh ... just thinking how my old man would be jumping up and down if he heard about our near miss today. It's bad enough that I sometimes climb without a rope."

\*\*\*

As we pull into town I stare up at the grey rock wall that looms over our landscape. With the late afternoon sun hitting it, the vast rock surfaces reflect the light like a giant mirror. Only the deeper gullies, which slice through it here and there, are left in shadow. How many times have I climbed it in my imagination? Hundreds of times. In my dreams I am always climbing solo, without rope or aid. There is no one and nothing to slow me down, so I move swiftly up the smooth face. I am absolutely free.

The reality of course is very different. Usually when climbing the Wall I'm bogged down with rope, a climbing rack, and somebody yakking away at me. But come spring, end of April maybe, I'll be climbing my dream. Any spare time I have now goes into perfecting my climbing technique and reading about the Wall — who climbed it first, when, where ... down to the last detail. Nobody knows what I'm planning. And that's the way I want to keep it — for now.

"Hello, Jay ... are you with me?" Brad's voice comes in. I see his hand weaving across my line of vision. "I asked you a question."

"You did?" I stare at his gaunt body hunched over the steering wheel. Like a sudden blow to my head I see how changed he is from the guy I knew a year ago. No more raunchy jokes, no more famous, bite-sized grins. And he's become careless about so many things. Even his hair that he used to dye a brilliant red is fading. Yeah ...

grey is the word that comes to mind as I watch Brad. He's faded to grey.

The truck hits the curb and stalls in front of his place.

"I was asking if you'd come in, Jay."

"Sure, why not. Which reminds me, I better dig the Iceman's stuff out of my pack."

Brad kicks a wheel of his pickup as he climbs out. "I'll have to sell the truck before it dies completely. I can't afford to keep it running."

"How will you get to Whistler then?"

Brad shrugs. "We'll see. Maybe get a lift with one of the guys from the High Rise here, when it works."

Ah yes, the Hilton High-Rise — the notorious two storey junker on the edge of town, home to a bunch of extreme sport types — all guys. I can hear my dad's voice lecturing me. "Steer clear of that place, Jay. It has a bad reputation. They do drugs there."

I know the crowd who hangs out at the High-Rise and they aren't all bad. Brad moved in when his parents split up and you could hardly describe him as dangerous, except to himself maybe. There are a few insane types, no question, but it's all about sports. One guy did anything that involved falling through thin air — paragliding, skydiving, parachuting — you name it. He dropped himself into a limestone crater, middle of the jungle somewhere in South America. They never found his body. The newspapers got their story, but with the wrong ending — for him at least.

Brad, who has been waiting patiently, pushes open the door of the High-Rise and I follow him inside. Late Saturday afternoon — the crew is all here and the place reeks of beer, popcorn, and drying boots. In the High-Rise everyone has a role to play. The Iceman is sitting at the kitchen counter, drinking beer and whipping up a batch of chocolate chip cookies. As an ice climber, in tricky coastal weather conditions, he's the acknowledged master of fear. "Hey, Brad," he says. "Close call you had today, eh? Glad I could help you boys out."

"Oh ... right," Brad stutters. "Thanks."

The Friendly Giant wanders over and slaps me on the back. "How is the Kid today? Been putting up any more solo routes?

I shake my head. "Too cold."

Friendly is big brother to the crew here, until he steps on a snowboard and eats up the competition. If the weather looks iffy he warns the Iceman, "Be careful today. We'd miss you, not to mention your chocolate chip cookies."

Brad and I don't a hundred percent belong here. I'm the youngest and the only one still going to school and living at home. Still, I get respect for what I do — free soloing some pretty gnarly rock pitches. And Brad? The problem is he hasn't made the first rung in any one sport and he's feeling the pressure. If you live here, you'd better do well ... really well.

I'm trying to follow Brad upstairs when the Iceman intercepts me. Luckily he can't tower over me like he does over Brad, because I'm a good head taller than him. "Surprised to see you taking up ice climbing," he says.

"I'm not taking up ice climbing. You told Brad to come along. He didn't have a rope partner so he asked me."

"You two are lucky I was there with that top rope."

"We thanked you already, right?"

I find myself glancing around for Brad or some escape route, but the Iceman has me cornered. "There are rumours flying around that you have some climbing event in mind."

"Event? Katy and I have been planning a back-country ski traverse this spring if that's what you mean. And we might nail a few peaks en route."

The Iceman grins. "I'm talking about a solo climb somewhere."

I haven't told anyone about my plans to solo climb the Wall. He must be fishing for info. I shrug and say nothing.

"Well, keep me informed. You might be able to drag me along. We both know I'd be more reliable than your friend Brad."

"Brad is a great rope partner. He's never been into ice climbing, that's all."

No wonder Brad has problems dealing with this showman. I wrench myself away and lurch upstairs. I push aside some wet clothes dangling over the stairwell, almost trip over some stray climbing boots, and knock on Brad's door.

"That you Jay? Come on in."

I shove the door open and find Brad lying down, boots and jacket still on. "How come you took off and left me with the Iceman?"

"I needed to get rid of my gear."

"Oh sure ... and I find you flaked out here. What is this, feeling sorry for yourself or something?"

Some of the old fire flashes in Brad's eyes. "No way. Matter of fact, I'm working on a plan."

"Thinking of moving out of here?" I ask hopefully. "Maybe you could bunk down at my place until something better comes along."

"You know I'm stuck here because it's cheap. About all I could afford is a shack in the woods or a tree house somewhere."

"But it's no good for you. Neither of us fits in here."

Brad's face screws up like a bulldog's. "About this plan I mentioned ..."

"Can you save it? I need to head home. It's my sister's birthday dinner tonight and I'm already late."

"Oh right. Wouldn't want to keep the family waiting. I'll tell you about the ski jump some other time."

A shiver like an icy glacial stream slides down my back. "But you've never been into ski jumping, Brad."

"I'm not talking about an ordinary ski jump — this will be a jump with a twist."

"What do you mean?"

"I need to do something that'll make people stop and stare. Look at what the other guys around here are up to."

"Yeah, I'm looking. And what's so great? The Iceman and the rest of them are just ordinary guys, no better than you."

"You're so wrong. They are all doing extreme stuff. They have reporters knocking on the door, sponsors, magazines asking for stories — most anything they want."

I'm hearing Brad, but it's hitting my ears with a hollow thud. He has to get out of this place. It's killing him, even though the guys living here aren't out to get him. Death comes in a hundred ways, I think. Sometimes quickly, sometimes step by step. When I first started rock climbing with Brad two years ago, he was upbeat. He had a girlfriend, plans for the future. And now? The shadow that I see darkening his face now as I say goodbye is there more often than not. He doesn't follow me downstairs.

"See you next week, Jay?"

"Sure." The word tumbles out and falls flat on its nose. I'll probably be too busy with school and Katy and everything. I can't keep track of him all the time, can I? Brad closes his door behind me.

Once outside I take the river road and begin loping towards home. It feels good to be away

23

from the High-Rise, breathing cool air again, catching the first drops of rain on my tongue.

As I run, my thoughts drift back to the frozen waterfall. How long before water will be plunging over the crest again? I think of Brad stalled beneath the ice bulge. His voice echoes in my ears, drowning out the explosion of crashing ice and cascading water.

# Chapter 3

After five days of pouring rain, Saturday morning opens with sunshine. I never did see Brad, never did manage to talk with him on the phone. One evening he left a message, but I didn't get around to phoning back. I should try and catch him this weekend. Trouble is he's either working or at the High-Rise, and I'm not supposed to be hanging out there. We used to be regular climbing partners until Katy came along. I've asked him to come with us so many times, but he always turns down the invite. Says something dumb like, "I'd only get in the way, or you guys don't want me around."

Brad is way off the mark there. You never forget a guy who's been on your rope, especially if he's rescued you from a crevasse. I remember how we were cruising along on our skis, unroped because the glacier seemed safe, and suddenly I was gone — two metres down in a hole. If not for Brad I might still be down there.

As I tuck into my usual bowl of granola, I smile at the weather outside and shut the door on Brad. I have to be at the Bluffs in an hour. I'm meeting Katy beneath Bare Bones, one of the tougher climbing routes there. I've soloed it twice, but it's new to Katy. Now that the rain has stopped, it should be dry.

My mom and sister have left for early morning aerobics, so it's just dad and me at the table. As usual dad is buried in his newspaper and only comes to life when I push back my chair.

"Climbing today, Jay?" he asks.

"Heading to the Bluffs," I say, ready for the usual interrogation.

"With a rope and some climbing gear, I trust?"

"Minimal hardware, maybe a chock or two, but definitely a rope."

"With whom, if you don't mind my asking?"

Yes, I do mind, but ... "Katy," I tell him.

"Good. I'm not happy when you are off climbing with that fellow from the High-Rise — Brad."

"He's all right."

"I don't care if he's all right. Is his equipment all right? I saw his rope once and it looked suspicious. And is his experience all right? Has he ever taken an avalanche awareness course, or a wilderness first aid course or ..."

"Dad, he's been climbing way longer than me."

"It's that whole High-Rise bunch I worry about,

the extreme stunts they keep dreaming up. Like careening down a seventy-degree gully on skis. You call that a sport? I call it attempted suicide."

"So why not complain about the suicidal drivers on our highways, Dad?"

"You have me there, Jay."

My dad finally lightens up and retreats to his newspaper. I grab a quick lunch and stuff it into my pack along with a climbing rope, a few slings, a chock or two — more to please Katy than anything else.

"Have a good time and be careful," my dad calls as I head for the door.

I let him have the last word. Then I'm off to the Bluffs, soaking up the sunshine as I go and studying the massive rock wall that looms overhead. You can see the Wall from all over our town. And it's big in my own head. I'm planning to climb it in late April, about the same time as the two guys who first made it up. The big difference is, they took weeks and I'm going to do it in two hours, max.

As I wander up the shortcut to the Bluffs, I puzzle over my dad's words. *Sport? I'd call it attempted suicide.* That's what he might say about my planned climb. But he's dead wrong. What's extreme for one person is a piece of cake for somebody else. It all depends on your training and skill level and how much you want to do something. I have plenty of the first two. Workouts at the climbing wall have turned me into a Spiderman clone. If you go without a rope, without any aid, you've got to move fast and you've got to be confident — that's the key. Not everyone can or should try it.

Yeah ... I can picture myself up there, the world at my feet. I'm tasting the first solo ascent of the Wall, and it's way better than hot chocolate after some iffy ice climb. No bolts, no cams, no chocks, no rope — just one, clean climb that no one else has done before.

*** 

When I reach the Bluffs I can't find Katy. Wonder why? She's always early. I grump around for a few minutes, finally pull on my rock shoes and dip my fingers into my chalk bag. Might as well warm up, instead of sitting around. I'm not wearing the new helmet my old man got for me. No one wears them here. It's not needed because the hundreds of climbers who work out here have swept the rock clean.

"But what about a rope?" My dad's voice echoes in my head.

"Don't need one. This climb is a breeze if you've taken the time to check it out beforehand."

I lean against the rock, letting the silence sink in, sweeping away any stray thoughts that separate me from the surface. I close my eyes. Stretch my arms until I feel like an eagle about to ride an updraft.

A slight overhang near the base starts me off. It's easy bouldering. I've done this hundreds of times. One quick arm movement and I've latched onto a rock nubbin above me. My height, all 190 centimetres of it, helps here. One leg straddles the overhang, the lower foot is smeared against the rough surface. Now I let myself glide over the rock. Sometimes when I'm alone I listen to my iPod, but not today because Katy is coming.

Before slipping into the diagonal groove that slices across the smooth rock face I dip both hands into my chalk bag. That'll take care of any sweat. I shake off the excess dust and let it drift to the ground below. At first the groove is large enough for a layback. With knuckles curled over the edge I walk myself up.

"Sweet," I murmur.

Where the groove narrows down to a mere scratch across the rock, I change my tactics. It's a bit dicier here, with only surface tension along the indentation to keep my feet moving. *Mind over matter,* my dad is always kidding me.

I start imagining myself as a river flowing over the rock. A river seeking out hidden notches and crevices, following every twist and turn, sweeping all before it. I am Jay, the riverman, scouring out my route, defying gravity. Unstoppable. Fingerholds and toeholds are my ladder to the sky. And I'm almost there

I see Katy below me, face upturned and watching. Knowing I'm concentrating on the next move, she doesn't speak or wave. Once she sees me sitting secure, feet dangling over the edge, she calls up, "Where's the rope? You promised me we'd use one."

"You weren't here. And I don't need a rope. I know this climb by heart."

"How come you didn't wait for me?"

"I did."

"Hardly. I'm only five minutes late." She sounds peeved.

"Sorry," I say. "Really. Grab the rope from my pack and head up the trail. I'll rig a top belay for you."

In a few minutes Katy is sitting beside me, feet dangling over the edge, too. The sun that is hitting our faces is warm for March. Across from us the Wall is still shadow, but the snow-covered mountains on each side shine with a blinding intensity. I risk draping one arm over Katy's shoulder. Lucky me today! For once she doesn't whisk my arm away like it's covered with germs.

"A perfect morning," Katy sighs.

Katy has called me her *climbing buddy,* ever since we met at the climbing wall last spring. I call her my girlfriend, but I know that's wishful thinking. Yeah, already my luck is running out — she whisked my arm off her shoulder.

"Yeah, not too bad a day," I mumble.

We couldn't be more different, the two of us. Katy is tiny and has short, curly hair as golden as the sun overhead. Everything about her is neat and compact. Me? I'm tall and scrawny, with too-long legs and a nose to match, and I keep swearing I'll mow down the black hair that flops over my fore-head. If you want to know the truth, Katy is so perfect she scares me. Guess I should be happy she tolerates me.

Of course the other major difference between us is that Katy is a total equipment freak. No way I can tell her about my planned solo climb. That could be the end of our climbing together, plus any chance of seeing her. I'm not about to take that risk.

I glance over Katy's shoulder, watching the sun's passage across the Wall's smooth, granite face. "Know why I was late?" Katy asks suddenly.

"No."

"Brad called. He said something about having the day off and you guys going ski jumping? When I told him you were meeting me here this morning you could have heard a feather drop. Not a word, he just hung up."

"I better go see him later today."

"Good idea. So what's with this ski jumping?"

"He hasn't told me much. I doubt it'll go."

"He sounded weird. How about we start climb-ing, so you can go see him soon?"

"I guess we better."

I start setting up an anchor for Katy's rappel rope. First comes the sling around our belay tree. Next I clip a locking carabiner into the sling and hitch the rappel rope into the 'biner. After this is done, I toss the rope over the cliff edge and watch it slither to the ground below. It's best to warn anyone standing there before you toss — ropes on the head are a no-no.

Now it's up to Katy. She stands on the edge of the cliff getting ready to rappel. After wrapping her rope around a figure-eight descender and clipping in, she double-checks the connections before stepping backwards off the cliff. Talk about being careful! Dad would be happy. I watch her bounding down the face, finally coming to rest at the bottom.

When it's my turn I put another anchor sling around our belay tree and clip in. This sling is longer so I can move to the edge of the cliff and watch Katy while I belay her up. Working with ropes can be a pain, but it's the only way for a novice climber. I worry that some young kid will see me climbing without one and think it's the neat thing to do.

"On belay now," I shout down to Katy.

The rope vibrates in my hands as she ties into her harness. Much fussing around before she calls up, "Climbing."

There's not much for me to do while she is climbing, except watch her overhead rope, making sure it doesn't get in the way and keeping it reasonably tight. Not that Katy needs a rope here, but try to tell her that.

"I'm waiting for some fancy footwork," I tell her, and I'm not kidding. Katy glides over rock like a ballet dancer. The audience is me and I'm always dazzled.

She only stops once to call up. "Don't keep the rope so tight, Jay."

A few more graceful hand-over-hand motions, combined with an airy layback and she is up, not even out of breath. "Well ... how did I do?"

"You were brilliant," I say, plunking myself down, legs hanging over the edge.

"Really, you mean it?"

"Of course."

Katy will never believe she is a world-class climber. I could tell her this a hundred times. I pull her down beside me and whisper "You are great, understand?" She makes a face, but ends up smiling.

For a while we sit there and watch the scene around us. The Bluffs are crawling now with rock hounds and rookie climbers. Every so often a groan or swear word drifts our way. It's like watching a cartoon — heads pop up from nowhere, bodies fall into space, then reappear dangling on the end of a rope.

"So what about Brad?" Katy reminds me.

Yes, what about Brad. Time to head back to earth and check on my friend. I wish Katy wasn't always right.

# Chapter 4

After saying goodbye to Katy outside her place, I head towards the Hilton High-Rise. I don't bother hurrying because the rest of my Saturday is mapped out — first Brad, then homework. Not exactly fun.

A half block away and I can already hear music and voices coming from the High-Rise. There's an occasional thump as some body catapults off the mini climbing wall that decorates the living room. They ought to put thicker mats under the overhang. If nothing else it would muffle the sound of falling bodies.

Standing outside the open door, I'm almost blown over by the smell. It's a Hilton cocktail of sweat, climbing boots, wet clothing that won't fit in the dryer and the usual popcorn rolling from the automatic popper. I take a final, deep breath before entering. The outside air reeks of river, exposed tidal flats and the distant pulp mill — the usual coastal perfume. It almost drowns out the stink of the Hilton High-Rise.

I lift my face to the mountains where the last colour is easing out. If I could be anywhere right now it would be up there with Katy, in my little tent with the quiet and the stars leaning down. Our skis would be there, too, stuck into the snow, waiting for the first morning light. We'd holler *Yeehaw* as we schuss straight down the slope, knowing a pancake breakfast is waiting in town.

Yeah, I have quite the imagination. And as my mom is always saying, "You have a wonderful way with words, Jay."

Oh sure, I've written a few poems and articles for our local *Alpine Club Journal*, but in the big world, competition is stiff. How many hundreds of guys out there are struggling to write the ultimate extreme sport story? Climb the highest peak on every continent, trek alone to the North Pole, ski or board down some sheer north face. Something tells me that if I quit school to climb and write the *big* story, my mother wouldn't think it's so wonderful.

Once inside, the rush of beer-soaked air hits my nostrils. "Hi Jay-walker," someone calls out. "What's the Kid been up to, more skipping school? Put up any gnarly, new solo routes?"

I grin sheepishly. "Yes, to the first question. No to the second." As the kid around here, I'm expected to do well, just not *too* well.

When the Friendly Giant claps me on the back, I collapse to the floor and play dead. He shakes a muscular fist over my upturned face and plays the teacher role. "Don't forget your schooling, son. We're counting on you to write us up when we make it to the Olympics."

Eventually I pick myself off the floor and grab my usual handful of popcorn. Everyone, except the Iceman goes back to drinking beer, waxing skis and snowboards, playing cards ... whatever they were doing before I wandered in.

"How is the climbing going?" he asks. The Iceman is checking me out with his frozen stare. "You never did tell me exactly what you're up to."

"Just the usual."

"Soloing?"

"Now and again. I spent the morning on the Bluffs."

"Did you red point any new routes?" More Iceman jargon.

"Not really. I free soloed Bare Bones for the second time. It's a breeze once you've done it."

"I was there this morning too. Didn't see you, though."

"No?"

"I've been hoping to run into you. Spider over there has been talking about putting up a new route on the Wall. He's looking for a rope partner. Any interest?"

"Me?" I hear myself squeaking.

"Sure, I was thinking you might ..."

Before he can finish, Friendly grabs him by the collar. "I go to wash a beer mug and what do I find? Spaghetti in the sink, spaghetti down the drain, spaghetti everywhere. Go get your ice pick."

"My ice picks are not plumbing tools. I hate water."

"I don't care what you like." Friendly drags him across the living room floor to the kitchen sink.

I turn away from the Iceman and the spaghetti fiasco and that's when I see Brad. He is sitting apart, his head buried in the usual outdoor magazine. He looks smaller and more ingrown than usual.

"How's it going?" I ask, sitting down beside him.

"Not much happening." Brad closes his magazine and leans closer to make himself heard above the noise. "Actually Jay, what I told you isn't a hundred percent."

"Oh?"

"Remember when we were together last and I mentioned ski jumping?"

"Of course I remember, Brad."

"Just wanted to make sure. You always seem to be in a hurry nowadays. I never know if you're listening."

"What do you mean?"

"I mean ..." Brad pauses and gives me the sad dog look that has been hanging around his face recently. "What I really mean is you don't have time for me. I'm not the funny guy anymore, cracking jokes and making you laugh. Right? So you've moved on."

"Look, I'm in big trouble for skipping classes. I shouldn't be here. Right now I should be at home doing chemistry."

"What, you haven't forgotten your old climbing partner?"

"Quit it, Brad. Let's get on with your story."

"Sure, anything you say ... Anyhow, since I talked to you last I've been working on my ski jumping technique. I'm pretty good."

"But you've never been into jumping. It's always been racing. You were aiming to be another Crazy Canuck and make the Olympics." Maybe the Crazy Canucks are history now, but around the Hilton their downhill races are still talked about with reverence. "Sure, point your skis downhill like them and go full out — it's a blast right?"

"Crazy Canucks? Not a chance. I haven't got their concentration. When you start watching the scenery go by, you're a no-go from the start."

"I don't get it. I can't think of anything that demands more concentration and nerve than ski jumping. I couldn't do it."

"Coming from you, Jay, that's a laugh."

"I dunno. The idea of falling through thin air with two boards locked to my feet. Nah-uh."

"What I'm planning isn't an ordinary jump." His eyes dart around the room and focus on the Iceman and the crowd bending over the kitchen sink.

"Go on, Brad."

Finally he whispers. "I can't tell you anymore now, Jay. This has to stay between the two of us until I have the details, worked out. Okay?"

"But you haven't told me anything new. I know nothing, apart from the fact you plan some ski jump."

"Come with me next week and you'll see exactly how and where I'm staging this event."

"Event!" I groan hearing the word again. What kind of circus is this?

"You'll come, Jay?"

"Sure, if it's the only way I'll find out what you're planning. But it'll have to be on a weekend. I can't skip any more classes. Which reminds me," I say, getting up from the grungy sofa, "I have to head home and study. Piles of catching up to do."

"Let me know when," Brad calls after me.

Before I can escape, Friendly steps off his homemade balancing board and intercepts me. He closes the door behind us. "Not good," he says, shaking his big, shaggy head. "What can we do about him?"

"You mean Brad?" I ask unnecessarily.

"Come evening he just sits here and vegetates. You think he's depressed or something? It's gotten much worse lately."

"I know. He's been down ever since his family split up. And living among you guys ... well, I guess he feels like a failure."

"I don't think so. Ever watch Brad working at the beginners ski lift — how he helps a kid who has fallen, takes the time to dust the snow off him? That guy's no failure."

"But he isn't good enough at any one thing. He'll never make it big time in the sport's world." Big time — yech! I hate my own words.

"Well, I'm worried about him. You know him better than anyone, Jay-walker. Try and talk to him." Friendly whaps me on the back, then goes back in and closes the door.

I check my watch. Quarter to eight. I should be at home doing chemistry, but I'm thinking about Brad and Friendly and that word, failure. Like a top rope slung over a cliff edge, I swing back and forth — go and talk to Brad now. No forget it. I should go back in there. But I'm a coward, the idea of a heart-to-heart with that screwed-up guy is way more daunting than any 5.11 rock pitch.

I take the long way home, following the river trail. I hear the current chewing at the bank, pulling pebbles, sand and the occasional boulder, after it. My thoughts seesaw with the river's eddies and rapids. Why rock the boat? Brad can figure things out for himself. But what if he needs help? The river churns back, *Men may come and men may go, but I go on forever.* Lines from a poem we read at school last week. Big deal. Still, the words haunt me, follow me home, long after I've left the river.

*** 

Voices jump on me when I reach home. First my mom. "We've all had dinner. I put yours in the oven, Jay."

"Sorry I'm late, Mom. It smells great." Not all that hungry — ate too much popcorn.

Next, my dad — totally predictable. "If you need some help with your chemistry, let me know." Gentle hint, this.

"Thanks, Dad, I'll wrestle with it after dinner."

Last, but never least, my sister. "I bet you've been at the Hilton High-Rise again."

"So?"

"You're not supposed to go there."

"Who says?"

"Everybody."

"Why don't you mind your own ... business?" I leave out the four-letter word that jumps to mind. She gives me a funny "yikes" look, as if she knows what I'm thinking. I head upstairs.

"Will you and Katy take me next time you visit the climbing wall?" she calls after me.

I stop halfway up the stairs. "If you promise to quit nagging me."

"As long as you promise to take me, I promise."

We both end up laughing. As younger sisters go she isn't too bad.

# Chapter 5

The end of March, beginning of April is a washout — literally. It rains as if the sun was non-stop slurping up the Pacific Ocean and dumping it overhead. The clear periods are so brief you might miss them if you blink an eye. As if this isn't enough, I catch the flu. It lays me low and puts me out of the climbing scene for a week or so. Every few days Brad calls me. He's anxious about everything it seems — the site where he plans his big ski jump, if and when I can come to look at it, weather, the snow level, timing of the event ... on and on it goes. I feel rotten and my patience wears thin.

Finally towards mid-April the weather breaks and so does my flu. Brad calls. "How about it? The weather looks perfect. Pick you up Saturday morning, say ten o'clock?"

I can think of things I'd rather be doing than sitting in a beat-up pickup truck on a beautiful

Saturday morning, but it's good to be up and about. And it'll give us a chance to talk. I'm keen to see what Brad actually has in mind, even though I have my doubts about his so-called event. Seems the only way I'll find anything out is by going with him.

As we head out of town and go north towards the town of Whistler, where Brad works, we're dazzled by our surroundings. It's like we've never seen these mountains before. During the last few days, the rain that practically drowned us down here was dumping snow on the peaks. Rising from the green valley they form a white rampart, appearing much higher than they really are. "They look like how I imagine the Himalayas or the Andes," I say.

"They sure do." Brad leans his head out the window for a better look.

"Why not turn into the viewpoint up ahead and stop for a minute? Be safer too."

"Still nervous from your near miss of a year ago, eh?"

"Sure am," I say. "The Iceman can't keep his eyes on the road, if there's ice anywhere. We're lucky we weren't pinned under that truck he veered into."

Brad stops the pickup beside the viewpoint sign, jumps out and starts reading aloud "This valley and the surrounding mountains were first ..."

"Spare us, will you?"

Brad is grinning from ear to ear. "I just love the way these guys describe our mountains."

"It's rich, all right."

We sit on the curb, letting our eyes skip over the peaks that fade into distant ice fields and blue sky. What's beyond the horizon still grips us. Brad and I were there once and made one incredible first ascent. I'll never forget the bushwhacking and the nail-biting climb over slippery rock and how darkness caught us on the way down. We had to spend the night without proper food or bivy bags. Whew ... but it was that feeling of standing on top that sticks with me.

"We should try and get up to the cabin this spring," I say finally, pointing across the valley.

"I'd like that," Brad says, getting up and opening the truck door.

We're on our way again. Like most of the High-Rise guys, Brad proceeds as if driving is just another extreme sport. If anything, today is worse than usual, because he's buoyed up by the weather and feels luck is on his side. Maybe it is, because we do reach the ski resort in one piece. Brad maneuvers the truck through the parking lot, past the lift where he works and onto an unploughed access road.

"Guess this is it," he says.

Can't say I'm sorry. After grabbing our skis from the back and attaching skins, we head up the road, Brad in the lead. I follow blindly, not knowing where or how far we are going. All I know is this: it's good to be breathing mountain air again, good to be feeling my legs and arms swinging as my skis float over the new snow.

"Spring skiing ... can't beat it!" I shout.

Brad turns around startled, then laughs. "Right on."

I'm hearing the old Brad in his voice. If he's this upbeat maybe the jump idea isn't so dumb, maybe he can pull it off and it'll be just what he needs.

Ahead where the grade is steeper, the road makes a switchback and cuts deep into the uphill slope. We go for maybe another fifteen minutes, until Brad calls a halt. "We have to cut up here, before the side bank gets too steep. It's not far now."

I study the slope looming overhead. "It looks pretty steep." This last winter has been a particularly heavy snow season, both here on the coast and in the Rockies. There have been several avalanche fatalities to date — three snowmobilers killed and two heli-skiers. I don't want to be another statistic, and I let Brad know.

But he assures me, "We can angle back across the slope where it's not so steep. This is the easiest spot to exit the road."

I pull my avalanche beacon from my pack and switch it on. "Let me know when you have yours turned on so we can check each other out."

Brad fumbles around his pack, coming up with slings, ski wax, first aid kit, camera and a few stale granola bars ... everything except his beacon. "I must have left it sitting by the front door."

"A lot of good it does sitting there," I grumble. "No use taking mine now. I guess we go without, if we go at all." Although my old man might think otherwise, I don't like taking unnecessary risks. I'm careful about what I do and stay within my limits. You listening somewhere, Dad?

I lift my ski pole and plunge it several times into the snow, gradually enlarging the hole. Too bad I didn't bring along my shovel so I could cut into the layers and do a proper avalanche test. "I dunno, Brad, it's hard to tell how well consolidated the snow is."

"Look, we've waited how long for a half-decent day? Let's go. And like I told you, we can angle back across the slope where it's not so steep."

"Okay, let's go." Neither of us wants to quit here and like Brad says it's probably safe. You can never be one hundred percent sure about a slope.

Brad takes the lead, heading back and across the slope as he promised. After leaving some distance between us, I start following his tracks. He's a strong skier and I soon find myself breathing heavily as I tramp along behind. I'm still out of shape after the flu. Every so often the snow underfoot settles with a loud *whumph*. Not sure I like the sound. I watch Brad's traverse, keeping an eye open for any telltale cracks in the snow.

"Stay where you are," Brad calls down. "I don't want you standing directly below me while I'm turning up here."

There are a few stunted trees poking through the snow where Brad is doing his kick turn. He probably figures it's safe enough with the trees holding the snow, but you can't always count on that. I once saw an avalanche roar through a spruce forest.

"Looks all right to me," Brad calls down. "I'll traverse back and gradually up. The snow is wind-blown ahead. I can see a rock sticking out."

Windblown ... chunks of crust coming loose? Not always good news, but if there isn't too much snow hanging there, it's probably fine. For a few seconds I pause, watching his progress across the slope. Soon he'll be directly overhead. No point waiting around. As I'm moving my left ski forward I hear a crack and see the snow pulling apart beneath Brad's skis. "AVALANCHE!" Brad screams.

For an instant my world is frozen. Crack spreading, snow slipping away — gaining momentum and size too. Coming right at me ... a few seconds left to escape. Run clumsily, skins sticking. Stumble and almost fall. Jerk my gloves free from ski pole straps. Too late to loosen ski bindings. See a rock sticking out. Head there. It'll mark the spot if I get pulled under. NO ... don't get pulled under.

"STAY ON TOP!" I hear Brad again.

Snow ... everything explodes around me. Cold in nostrils, ears and eyes. Mouth too. Snow pulling at my legs — so heavy — snatching away hat, tossing skis about. It flows like a wild river, dragging me along. But I'm lucky. I manage to reach the edge. I swim with my arms and somehow keep afloat.

The avalanche chucks me aside like a piece of driftwood and finally my body stops moving. I lie face down in the snow. Below, I can still hear the onward rumbling of the beast as giant snowballs twist and turn. But I'm on top. I can breathe! I spit the snow from my mouth.

Slowly, I untwist my skis, straighten out my legs. Nothing is broken. My hat is within reach, my gloves are only half buried. Poles? Probably somewhere below me caught up in all that mess. Lucky if they aren't broken. I can see one down there, sticking out like a toothpick. I stand up and shake the snow from my hair. If the avalanche had dragged me under I'd be frantically trying to clear a breathing space around my face before the snow hardened. I'd be fighting panic, trying to conserve air. Wondering which way is up or down, stunned and confused. I reach for my hat. Notice my hands are shaking. Hat ends up lopsided. Like everything else right now. The sound that spills from my throat is shivering too. I'm laughing crazily ...

More shouting. "Jay, can you hear me?"

My eyes are riveted on the jumbled snow mass below me. The avalanche has swept the slope clean and spilled across the access road. The snow must be several meters deep down there.

If I'd been further along in Brad's tracks, I'd be down there too — no avalanche transceiver beeping out my whereabouts.

"Jay!" It's Brad calling again. He's standing directly above the spot where the avalanche ripped loose and swept the slope bare. Imagine a figure standing at the apex of a triangle and you've got the picture. I watch him push off, schuss down the avalanche track and sideslip to a stop beside me. "You're okay? Nothing broken?" The words tumble out.

I shake my head. "You didn't have to ski all the way down."

"You think I'd just leave you? For a minute there I thought you had been dragged under."

"It was close. I got rolled off my feet."

"Sorry, Jay. I feel rotten about forgetting my transceiver. I was in a hurry this morning and the Iceman kept yakking as I was leaving."

"Forget it, Brad. No one got hurt. But it sure is a lesson in having the right gear along."

Brad nods and hands me half an orange and one of his stale granola bars. "Eat. Then we can decide what's next."

While I'm working on Brad's granola bar I study the place where the avalanche broke loose. It started small, then took a huge chunk of the slope with it. Not much left to come down. Brad is watching my every move. The granola bar is one of the chewy kinds. By the time I'm finished it feels like half my teeth are missing.

"What do you think? Are you into going on?" Brad asks.

"Why not, you want to show me your jump site, right? Plus we don't have to worry about all that snow up there 'cause it's … down there.

"I'll go collect your poles. Try moving your legs around, make sure everything is all right."

"Don't worry, doc, I'm fine. And thanks to your granola bar even my teeth have quit chattering."

Brad claps me on the back as he heads down to find my two ski poles. "Thanks for doing this, Jay," he calls.

"No prob."

Later, we wind our way back up as the sun slowly spreads across the slope. When it reaches us we stop to take off our wind jackets, stripping down to a bare minimum. The warm April sun scatters any chill left by the avalanche.

"Weather couldn't be more perfect if we ordered it," Brad says.

"Uh-huh." I'm not in talking mode. Too busy catching my breath.

We are following a flat shelf that stretches across the slope and ends in an obvious high point. Underfoot the snow is becoming softer, occasionally sticking to our skins if we pause or lift our skis. With each stride we take, balls of snow take off, gathering momentum until they reach the steeper section swept bare by the avalanche.

New snow, and now with sun beating down — even without our added weight that slope would not be healthy. It's probably a good thing the snow took off when it did. At least we'll be breathing easier skiing back down.

I stop for a rest and let Brad pull ahead. His ski poles are flashing in the sunlight. I can't believe how eager he is. Is this the same shriveled-up guy I saw at the High-Rise? At the top he turns and waves so I take off up the slope after him.

"What's next?" I ask, drawing up beside him.

"This is it."

From my vantage point I'm seeing snow-covered mountains across the valley and trees marching down the steep sides to where the ski village is nestled. Scenic, all right. But Brad is not looking there. His gaze is focused on the slope directly below us. It's hard to gauge the steepness of a slope when you're standing at the top. All I know is, the angle looks too steep — maybe 50° at the top, then levelling off before the road.

I turn to Brad, looking for an explanation. "So?"

Brad leans over one ski and frets it back and forth. Doesn't look me in the eye. "Yeah ... so I ski down the slope, getting enough speed and lift to clear the road, plus the tower on the other side."

"That's it?"

"More or less. And I'm counting on you to take some photos as I'm jumping."

"Brad, I'm an amateur photographer. You need a professional if you want to make the newspapers, magazines ... whatever."

"I don't have any media contacts. What about

that guy from the city who interviewed you after your first solo climb?"

"That was ages ago, Brad. I don't even know if he still exists. Why not talk to one of the High-Rise types? They hit the news often enough."

"Yeah, I should do that."

"Look ... have you thought this thing through properly? I'm wondering if there's enough story here to grab the media's interest. It has to be something pretty big, you know."

Brad keeps looking down the slope, as if he hasn't heard my question.

I follow his gaze down the shimmering snow slope. It looks perfect, untouched by ski tracks, each snow crystal reflecting its own special shape and beauty. Why go and change the picture, I wonder? What I don't like, and I'm eyeballing it now, is the road cut. Hard to tell from here how deep or wide it is. And worse than that — the far embankment. It's a rock tower. The snow has melted there, except for a few icy patches. Brad has to clear that gnarly tower before hitting the downslope, or else ...

"Have you checked everything out, Brad?"

"You mean like my take-off point, distance across the road?

"Sure. And all the other equations like snow conditions, wind, and air temperature. And what about skis? Have you got a decent pair of skis, something that will work for jumping? And ski wax?" I can think of lots more questions.

"It's doable. And my old, long skis are working just fine. Too bad the snow conditions aren't better today. I would have tried a practice run."

"You would?"

"If I don't get up and running soon, weather will be too warm." Long pause. "You don't look exactly enthusiastic, Jay."

"I'm not. Like I said, Brad, I'm on shaky ground when it comes to jumping. Talk to Friendly. He's got the experience."

Brad shakes his head. "You keep telling me to talk to someone else and I probably will. But it's your support I need. And if I'm lucky you'll actually be listening."

That last bit from Brad hits me square in the chest. I'm listening, all right. And now, instead of the untouched surface, I imagine Brad hurtling down the slope. He loses balance where the slope levels off, then flies into space, becoming smaller and smaller until all I can see is a dot no bigger than a fly. I close my eyes, trying to shut off the image.

"Jay?"

"Yeah."

"What I need are spring snow conditions — freezing temperatures overnight and warmer days. The corn snow will give me speed without being too icy, right?"

"I guess."

"If things work out as planned I'll stage the jump sometime in late April. All I need is your help, Jay. You know ... checking out my equipment, just being there, maybe lending a hand with the media or helping me write up a story."

Here we go with the media again ... Sure, go out and kill yourself in some bizarre way and every newspaper in the country will come running. Over the last few years there have been some sensational jumps staged near here. One guy leaped off a sheer cliff; another almost got buried in the avalanche that followed him down. One story that made it into the news sticks in my mind. A young skier, about my age, tried to jump across a truck parked in the road. Didn't make it, and landed on the truck's roof. Though I try to shake off the image, all I can see is Brad hurtling through space, landing god knows where.

"Uh, Jay? How does April sound?"

"Not bad for snow conditions, but I don't think ..."

Brad breaks in. "And you'll be around?"

"Look, Brad — I want to help if I can. But from every angle, this jump is looking too risky. Why bother, man?"

Brad scrapes his skis across the snow, without looking up. "Do me a favour, will you Jay? Let me work on this plan. Sometime later we'll get together and toss it around. Then we'll tear it up, or not. Agreed?"

"Agreed." I'm off the rope and hanging free for the moment. With a shout I turn and point my skis down our uphill tracks. "Come on, before the snow gets too soggy."

Brad takes off after me. I can hear the zing of his skis, his breath rising as he chases me. Together we hit the top of the avalanche slope, crank a jump turn and carve figure eights across each other's tracks on the way down. "Yeehaw!"

This is how it should be — two friends laughing and luring each other on. Near the bottom we schuss full out then slide to a stop just short of the avalanche debris.

"Sweet." Brad smiles and wipes the melting snow from his face.

I do the same. And I let the rest go.

# Chapter 6

It's nearing the end of April, but it feels more like June. Temperatures have already hit the mid-twenties. While walking home from school, I've seen geese winging north and swallows balancing on telephone lines. Everything seems to be on the move. I feel that same pressure. Every afternoon while I'm exercising on the Bluffs I've been eyeing the Wall, asking myself the big question, "*When?*"

It's Tuesday now and if the weather holds, I'll go for it this coming Friday. I don't think this high-pressure system hanging over us will last through the weekend. If it does, the lower reaches of the Wall will be swarming with rock rats, and I don't want an audience. What I need is the space to concentrate on this, my biggest solo climb ever.

Over a late dinner Dad keeps grilling me about climbing. It's probably the good weather that has got him thinking about what I might be planning.

"How is the new climbing helmet I bought you working out, Jay?"

"Great, it fits perfectly."

"Yes, I know it fits. We tried it out together at the climbing equipment co-op, remember? The question is have you actually worn the thing while climbing?"

"For sure. I used it a couple days ago when I was scrambling up one of the Wall gullies. Lots of loose rock there."

Obvious look of relief on his face. "Glad to hear that. It's important to wear a helmet whenever there's a danger of loose rock."

"You're totally right."

Although the parental worrying grates on me sometimes, I shouldn't be too hard on the old man. He knows what mountains are all about. Objective dangers like rockfall, sudden weather changes, cornices collapsing from above, rogue avalanches — he's seen them all. So what can he do but keep nagging his sixteen-year-old kid and go buy him a better helmet?

"Any particular plans for the weekend, Jay?" my mom asks

"Not really. Are you guys thinking of something?"

"If the weather holds I was thinking we could do a back-country ski trip somewhere, all four of us."

"Great. Could Katy come too?"

"Of course, as long as her parents know what we're planning."

This is a sore point. Katy's folks are not climbers or back-country skiers, and they're super fussy and cautious. "I'll let Katy know what's up and she can talk to her parents."

"Be sure they are properly informed, Jay," my dad has to add.

"*Okay!*"

It's a good time to leave the table before people start asking about the rest of the week. I don't like the curious look in my sister's eyes or mom's sphinx-like stare. She's too good at mind reading. As I'm pushing my chair back the phone rings. Somehow I know it will be Brad.

"Can we meet somewhere, Jay?"

I'm feeling the pressure from all sides. "Can't you tell me over the phone or let it wait until tomorrow?"

"You know the phone is in our kitchen, Jay," he says in a barely audible voice. "I can't talk with everyone sitting around here. And tomorrow I'm working at the ski resort and won't be home until late Thursday night, more likely first thing Friday morning."

"Friday is no good for me."

"How about we meet now at Konnie's Kitchen? It's close. I'll buy you a coffee."

"You know I hate coffee."

"Well, whatever ... just come."

"I'll hop on my bike. Give me ten minutes."

"Thanks, Jay."

As I grab my jacket and head for the door my sister gives me her I-know-where-you're-going look. "I am not going to the Hilton High-Rise," I toss over my shoulder.

After the hassle of dinner with the family, it's good to be standing under a clear sky and breathing cool air. An almost full moon is lighting the Wall, making it appear even more vast and remote, if not untouchable. The dark lines of the gullies descend like spider legs onto the ground below. "Awesome," I whisper.

Through the lighted window of Konnie's Kitchen I see Brad's head bent over what looks like a well-marked notebook. He sees me, dips his finger in his coffee, and smears *Hi* on the glass. The waitress, seeing more work coming her way, gives him a dirty look. Gives me one too, as I enter.

"What have you got there, Brad?" I ask.

"A diagram of the jump site, showing the various angles. My takeoff point is a bit steep. I may have to shovel in some snow and level it off a bit." He marks an X on his notebook page. "But it's looking pretty good right now."

"Right now?"

"I'm planning to do my jump, or at the very least a dry run, for this weekend.

"Why this weekend, Brad?"

"Timing couldn't be better. A few days ago they ploughed the access road and the sun has melted any leftover snow. What do I see as I schuss down the slope? White snow, black pavement. There'll be no problem pinpointing my takeoff point."

Talk about timing — bad timing. My own climb is scheduled for Friday and Brad is set to go this weekend. The Wall and my planned route are clearly visible from all over town. Wham — instant news. How will it hit him? Especially if he sees me turning thumbs down on his own jump. And if I squash my own plans? Ah, it wouldn't change a thing. The guy is obsessed with his *event,* as he calls it.

I look up to see Brad staring across the table, his fingers tapping the notepad, which is lying open. "What do you say, Jay? Is it a go?"

"Let's have a closer look."

I pull the notepad over. On paper it looks like a child's doodle. He's drawn this stick figure hurtling down a slope. And yes, the angle is marked — approximately fifty degrees at the top, then levelling off where the figure becomes airborne. The sketch is so roughly drawn it takes me several minutes to figure everything out.

"Where's the rock tower on the far side of the road? I don't see it."

Brad jabs his finger at a minor bump. "Right here."

"Look, if you're going to do a diagram it's got to be accurate. Your tower isn't some puny pimple on the landscape. It's big." I grab Brad's pencil and add some height to the far embankment, colour in a few icy patches that I remember seeing. "There."

"Relax, man. I'm not doing a landscape painting."

I bend over his sketch again. A few pencil dots show what will probably happen — stick figure clears road and embankment, lands on downslope, and raises arms in triumph.

Brad, I'm thinking, this is not kid's play — this is the real world.

When I force myself away from the notebook, Brad is waiting for me, looking hopeful. "So?"

"Why the question mark over the road?"

"Because the distance across varies from place to place.

"Why not get the exact figure for your jump point?"

He shrugs. "It depends on where exactly I take off and how much wind there is. I know the approximate distance."

I tap the notebook. "Then write it down so you have everything in black and white. You said it yourself — white snow, black pavement. Better calculate it to the exact centimetre. Have you talked to Friendly or anyone else?"

"Not yet, but I'm planning to."

"It's already Tuesday. You better move, Brad."

"I might try a practice run tomorrow. I'll talk to him afterwards."

"Why wait till after. Are you going with anyone?"

"Not unless you feel like coming."

61

"I can't skip more classes." As I say this, I'm thinking guiltily of Friday. "You ought to have someone along."

"Don't worry. There's a good chance I won't have time for a practice run. It'll depend when I get off work."

I down the lukewarm hot chocolate that the evil-eyed waitress brought me and get up to leave. I've got to tell him — now or never. My voice is sounding hollow. "Remember when I said there's no way I'd try this jump myself?"

"Sure, I remember. You've said it more than once."

"I don't have the skill. With skill goes confidence."

Brad makes a face. "Gee ... thanks. You sound like you're reading from some self-help manual. What are you trying to say?"

"Don't try the jump, Brad. It's too risky."

Brad shuts his notebook. "I guess I needed to hear someone say the words. It's no great surprise."

"Sorry, Brad."

"Why sorry, man? You've got the guts to be honest. It's back to square one. I'm a failure at ski jumping, at everything."

"I never said failure."

"You don't need to. I said it." Brad drops some money on the table and gets up really suddenly.

The waitress is marching towards us, obviously wanting to close the place up. I grab Brad's arm as he makes for the door. "You can't just walk out."

"No?"

"Ski jumping isn't the end of the line, Brad. What about all those north faces in the Coast Mountains, just waiting for us to come along?"

"Sure, we'll talk about it sometime ... not now. I got to be up early. Some people have to work, you know."

I watch Brad slouch off to his truck and then I peddle off into the night, feeling the darkness pressing down on me. Is Brad the only one who changed? What about me? All I can think about these days is the Wall ... that Wall looming over me now. I blame myself. I blame Brad. I blame the Hilton High-Rise. Maybe I shouldn't have told Brad to junk his plan. I didn't want to, I kept putting it off. And now he's depressed. Brad and I have shared the same rope how many times? But does that make us good friends? What's a friend, then? I don't know the answer. Round and round I circle in the darkness.

The one thing I do know for sure is this, come Friday I'll be climbing the Wall — me, myself and I. "Solo!" I shout into the night. And screw the consequences.

# Chapter 7

Awake? Asleep? I don't know. I'm hearing myself ... somebody, shouting. Or maybe I've been dreaming the sound which is slowly fading away. My mouth is open and panting like a dog's after the chase. My eyes are staring, but I see nothing. It's dark as a bat's ear in my bedroom this early Friday morning — Wall Day as I've come to call it.

"What time is it?" I wonder, groping under the bed where I've stashed my alarm clock.

My dream — better call it a nightmare — is still gripping me. I'm watching from above as Brad starts up the last rock pitch. "Nah, this is easy," he says. "Don't bother belaying." So I don't.

The rope lies in careless coils beside me. Brad is smiling. Then without warning, without a sound, he falls backwards, arms and legs splayed out as if doing a cartwheel. In slow motion he drifts away from me, tumbling end over end in space. The rope unravels through my fingers and hands. I try to tighten my grip on it. But I can't ... I can't.

Fumbling for the alarm, my fingers feel helplessly stiff. I must have been lying the wrong way. Aah, finally found it. Four o'clock. Another hour to go.

I groan and collapse back on my bed, hoping sleep will come. No use. I can feel my eyeballs swivelling back and forth, keeping time with my thoughts. It's too early to start off. Besides I need the shut-eye, there's a big day ahead. Could anyone believe that falling asleep was such a chore?

And talking of chores, it's been a non-stop sweat keeping this climbing project under wraps. I've told no one. If Katy suspects anything, she hasn't let on. Sure, I've been methodical — with the old man on my case I have to be careful. My clothes, lunch, and books are all laid out for school today. Climbing gear, what little I need, is stashed away in my cupboard. If any news were to leak out beforehand, my plans would be good and drowned, plus my dad's blood pressure would soar. Once I'm on the Wall, someone is bound to spot me. But they can't stop me. And the consequences? I'm trying to blank that from my mind ... for now.

"Whew." I try lying on my back and covering my eyes with both hands. Sleep won't come. I can't even relax. Thoughts keep pouring out like coins from a slot machine.

I can hear my dad's voice lecturing me, "You climb with ropes and another experienced climber. But you want to go alone, without a rope, without any equipment? Crazy."

"Uh-oh," I hear footsteps tromping down the hall. A door opens and shuts. The toilet flushes. I hear a sneeze outside my door — a real dad trumpet. Just what I need. "Go back to sleep, Dad," I whisper wearily. I need to be up in fifteen minutes.

I lie here, like a half-dormant cocoon, listening for the slightest sound. Five minutes ... ten minutes go by. I wonder if he's snoring yet. When will it be safe to move?

"Think Wall," I tell myself. "Sweep your mind clear of everything else."

I've been gripped by this sheer rock face ever since I was a kid and read about the two guys who first climbed it back in the sixties. Most of their story I know by heart. How every day they climbed and every evening they rappelled back down, leaving their fixed ropes. Same old grind, over and over. How they drilled over 100 rock bolts when there were no handy piton cracks, where they rappelled off the face so they could spend the night below, which ledges they bivouacked on when they were nearing the top and could no longer rappel off the face ... even down to the rat and the mosquitoes that plagued them one sleepless night.

It was one incredible feat for those early days. Guess everyone else thought so too, because one weekend thousands of cars jammed the highway below, everyone wanting to watch the crazy climbers. The guys started the climb in May and finished mid-June. Of course, they weren't climbing steadily like I'll be doing. I mean they even had to hack out a trail to reach the base of the Wall. Setting up their fixed ropes took time too — something I sure won't be worrying about. Plus, they were exploring a new route. Nowadays climbers scramble up the Wall in a day. Me? By free soloing it I aim for two hours — max.

Three minutes to five. Time to stir. I lean over and switch off the alarm before it has a chance to go off. My brain is spinning like an outboard motor. Round and round we go. Now I'm wondering if this sleep loss will cramp my climbing style. Worry, worry, early morning craziness.

When my feet hit the floor, all ten toes curl up like caterpillars from the cold. Can't see where I left my socks. I switch on my headlamp for a second and the room comes into focus. I turn it off, after pulling on my climbing pants and shirt and retrieving my day pack. I stand motionless, listening for any sound. Nothing. Great!

Now comes the risky part — leaving my room. I open the door a crack and hold my breath before pulling it wider. Good, not a peep from my parents' room. I tiptoe down the stairs, being careful to skip the step that squeaks, then stop by the front door to pull on my hiking boots. So far, so good. A rush of cool air hits my face as I open the door.

With both hands I pull it shut behind me, holding the knob so the latch doesn't click too loudly.

Although I'm confident no one has heard me, I still find myself running down the road, my heart pounding. The cool air and sudden effort bring on a coughing fit. I lean over the pavement, gagging. "What's the big hurry?" I ask myself. I force myself onto the sidewalk, trying to walk like any sensible person would at 5:15 a.m.

Houses drift past. Here and there a light shines from a window — perhaps a logger going to work or someone heading into the big city. After cruising past the twenty-four-hour restaurant, where some all-nighter is bent over his coffee, I cross the main highway that goes past our town. A single car catches me in its headlights. A few more loping steps take me onto the gravel road leading towards the Wall. The rough ground feels good underfoot.

I've done it. Now that I'm not pounding pavement I feel my heart slowing down and my legs relaxing. The air smells good here — damp rock, last year's leaves squishing underfoot and the sharpness of balsam poplars hitting my nostrils. Yes, this is all right.

The road slopes up towards the Wall, ending in a turnaround, pitted with the usual garbage. You wonder why some jerks come all this way to dump their black plastic bags. A few beer cans wink back at my flashlight. As I expected there is no one about now. Later in the year this place will be swarming, even at such an early hour.

After picking up the well-worn trail, I turn off my headlamp. The darkness overhead is giving way to a bluish tinge and familiar shapes lurch from the shadows. Occasionally alder branches arching over the trail whip my face or a cobweb latches onto my hair — proof that no one else has walked the trail this morning.

The trail steepens and makes a switchback. Suddenly rock looms ahead. Not a boulder or two, but a vast rock face with only its feet showing. Though I crane my neck, I can't see the distant top — the angle is too steep. A wave of apprehension prickles the back of my neck and ripples down my body. The massive face towering overhead presses down on me.

Gingerly, I reach out and touch the rock, letting my fingertips rest there as if expecting the rock to move or speak. Nothing ... no voice echoes down, just a single drop of water hitting my head. For a moment I watch the sun waking the distant mountain peaks — grey shifts to pink, shifts to red, shifts to scarlet. "Hello, sun," I whisper. Below me, the valley bottom is still in a shadow.

It's been a long road to the base of the Wall here. It started when my parents tied me into a climbing rope at age three. Then I graduated to rock faces, indoor climbing walls and, best of all, the real mountains. Sure, they can lecture me as much as they want, but my parents got me going.

Get going! The two words shake me fully awake. I gulp down the peanut butter and jam sandwich I made last night and take a swig of water. I'm as ready for this climb as anyone can be. Last summer I climbed the Wall four times — twice with Brad, once with Katy, and another time with Friendly. But climbing it solo, minus any gear, has been my dream. Nobody has done it before. I stare up at the 460-metre rock face that is waiting there. Yes, it's time to climb.

# Chapter 8

I stand up and start dragging stuff from my pack. Apart from a few essentials like my chalk bag and a small, emergency water bottle, everything else will be left behind here. There's no choice. A pack could catch on something, upset my balance if it shifts. A chalk bag dangling over my behind is more than enough.

Conditions are perfect. A light breeze is brushing the rock face, drying any overnight moisture. Not too hot, not too cold. Because the Wall faces west it doesn't get sun until late morning. That's fine by me. I won't be baking in the sun and frying my fingertips.

As I pull on my special rock shoes I smile a bit smugly, thinking of the heavy boots those first pioneers on the Wall were wearing. I take another drink, not too much — I don't want to be stopping for a pee, especially when there aren't that many places to stop. Now it's sweater off, chalk bag fastened onto my waist sling.

I take a few deep breaths to relax and reach my arms overhead and place my palms on the Wall. The coolness of the rock flows down my arms. For a moment I hesitate before the rhythm of climbing takes over. My mind focuses on the rock staring me in the face. Everything else gradually fades out — the hum of traffic from the highway, a horn honking somewhere, a faraway boat whistle.

My fingers creep like spider legs towards a crack that breaks the smoothness of the rock. Finding it, they crawl inside, expanding and wedging themselves firmly there. The crack's sharp edge has torn my skin. I don't feel any pain and keep moving but blood oozing from one finger stains the grey rock and has made my hands slippery. Trying not to stop my upward momentum, I dip each hand quickly into my chalk bag. There is no substantial hold here. I have to keep moving. I can't afford to pause and break my rhythm. Up I go, grabbing, bracing myself, straining every muscle in my body, using every bit of roughness on the rock's surface. My breath comes evenly. The air is cool and damp and smells of rock. It's good.

"Damn." My fingers bump into a piton — a knife blade some climber hammered in and left behind. Junk protection, I think. It's blocking my best hold in the crack here. Can't touch it if I say I'm climbing without aid.

I'm forced to stop and shift balance, losing my upward momentum. I move my right hand above the piton, leaving the fingers of my left hand jammed into the crack below. Both feet are balancing on small rock nubs. It's at least thirty metres clear to the ground. Already my calf muscles are trembling from the strain.

I crawl my left hand over the piton, wedge my fingers into the crack above. I've got them buried up to the knuckles. They are like tiny posts, binding me to the rock. Now draw the right leg up — easy, don't rush it. "Ahh," my right foot finds a rock nub and the pressure eases.

Not far above me, I see the first decent ledge where I can stop and grab some trail mix. I could sure use some water. I've already cranked out enough sweat to make my mouth go dry.

Above the piton, the crack becomes more negotiable. I sail through it and within minutes am pulling myself onto the ledge. It's wide enough to have a small tree growing on it. Those first two climbers, and how many others since, have anchored their ropes to it. On closer inspection I can see rope marks creasing the bark. I pat the trunk. "Not to worry. I won't be hanging any ropes today."

Other than coarse grass and moss where moisture seeps out, the ledge is bare. Look over the edge here and all you see is empty space. I know a few people, my sister included, who wouldn't like the view.

After a drink of water, I turn my attention to the so-called flake chimney directly overhead. The climb itself won't be difficult, probably an easy class 5 in climbing jargon. What isn't so nice is the water seepage, which is always a problem here in spring. I draw my fingers across a greasy-looking rock surface. It's slippery and I'll have to go easy here.

The chimney is more like a deep groove in the rock, a place where I can wedge a foot and occasionally a shoulder to brace myself. This is one place where being tall and skinny comes in handy. For a guy as big as Friendly, it's a tight squeeze. Like some gigantic, prehistoric worm I squirm my way upwards.

Where the chimney ends, I pause and glance up. The real climbing begins here. A smooth, grey wall is looming over me, broken only by a series of vertical rock fissures and impressive v-angles that go soaring into the blue above me. Dihedrals, dad calls them. There lies my route for the next two hundred metres or so. The almost flawless face is awe-inspiring. No messy little cracks split the surface, not many rock nubbins either. I've been here a few times, and I'm always gripped by the same feeling — call it terror if you like.

I've been going for less than an hour. Won't be long until I'm standing on top, soaking up the sunshine. Sure ... but don't go jumping ahead of yourself, Jay. What I need to do now is deal with these greasy hands. First I rub both palms across my already filthy pants, then plunge them into the chalk bag. If I ever needed a dependable grip, it's now.

I watch the stray chalk dust drifting down into the empty space below me. "Gone," I hear myself whisper. Can't help but feel the sheer magnitude of this place. I wouldn't mind if Katy was here, even my old man. I smile at the thought of my dad up here. It wouldn't be his cup of tea as he likes to say. No, he definitely would not get it.

Before moving onto the face I shut my eyes and listen to the wind, a raven's craggy call as it catches an updraft, water dripping down a nearby chimney. Okay, I'm ready.

The rock flake I'm eyeing juts out a few centimetres from the face proper, forming a perfect angle where climbers have placed hundreds of bolts, pitons, cams and chocks over the years. This is my line too, minus the usual hardware. I anchor my hands behind the rock flake, lean back on my arms and walk my feet up. A perfect layback. I'm a fly walking up this wall. My legs and hands are glued to the surface. I can hang upside down, move up, down — anywhere I want. I do everything but buzz. "Yeehaw!"

I've tuned into the rhythm and I'm dancing with the wind and that old raven bird overhead. Nothing can stop me now. I'm nearing the top of what climbers call the Split Pillar. Won't be a problem like it was for those first two climbers, because I'm not using pitons. The rock flake they were working on all those years ago, kept splitting further from the main wall as they hammered in pitons. A lower piton actually popped out while the upper one was being driven in. Luckily the lead guy was already clipped, in or else ... I don't want to think about it, not while I'm this far off the ground. "Focus on the rock," I whisper to myself.

What I'm seeing as I crane my neck upwards is a massive rock flake jutting out from the Wall. Like some giant sword, it's aimed directly at me. My gaze is drawn into the black hollow beneath that flake. Don't stay there, Jay. Your way is up and over.

I hear my heart beating. Or is it the sound of the rock? Older climbers have told me the rock flake here actually vibrates like some giant gong when pitons are being hammered in. I imagine tense voices nearby, the ringing *boing boing* of pitons.

"Go, Jay." I mumble. I force my feet higher. I picture them as tentacles, little suction cups latching on to the surface. My fingers curl over a rock edge, scratch across grass and grab a shrub. It's solid. I pull myself onto a prominent ledge that slices across the Wall and smell the good smell of terra firma. Terra firma? Depends on your perspective. Distance-wise, I'm three quarters of the way, but I'm a mere speck plastered against the Wall. Leaning over the ledge I look straight down, 370 metres more or less to the *real* terra firma.

Although the sun isn't hitting the Wall yet, the air is definitely feeling warmer. I dangle my feet over the sloping ledge and let the breeze run around my legs. It feels good after the workout I've had. I reach around to retrieve my small water bottle. Where it should be attached to my sling, there is nothing. I must have left it on the first ledge. And I'm the one saying Brad is careless. Idiot!

Suddenly the day feels much warmer. My mouth is as dry as a camel's nostril, so dry I can't even spit my disgust over the edge. Funny coincidence that the two guys who first climbed the Wall ran out of water around here, too. Not funny, actually, because after a couple of nights spent on the face, they were suffering severe dehydration and made some bad mistakes.

Leaving my water bottle behind isn't the end of the line. But I gotta be careful. I don't have a rope or any backup, so even a small mistake can be fatal. I can't rappel back down and I don't have anyone to drag me up. I'm alone. And I'm thirsty and hungry and I'm standing on the edge of an impressive drop. Well, too bad, Jay. You wanted to go it alone.

I lean against the rock, which feels cool and slightly damp. But running my tongue across the surface doesn't ease my thirst. Can't eat much, because the handful of trail mix I brought along is too dry and salty. "Quit whining," I tell myself. "It'll be fine." When I reach the top, I can run down the backside trail to the stream. There's maybe 100 metres to go. I decide to end this climb before my muscles start cramping. To loosen up I swing my arms around, letting them smack against my legs. Then I start climbing again.

I find myself directly below a giant boulder that is wedged into a chimney. With a jolt, I recognize the spot — I've been moving more quickly than I thought. Brad and I usually rig up the chockstone here with a few slings and use it as a bombproof belay for the lead climber. Seeing as the crux of the whole climb lies ahead, this is a smart move

Today I'm on my own, so I do things differently. I grip the chock stone in a huge bear hug and ease myself up and over. Quick and easy. Foolproof too, eh Dad? With both feet planted firmly on the boulder, I take a moment to survey my kingdom. I'm the eagle, I'm the raven, I am the Kid. "Yahoo!"

Time to take off. I arch my back, forcing every muscle to propel me upwards. Legs are spread-eagled in the chimney, arms are extended overhead like overworked rubber bands.

Directly above me is the crux — a sheer flake of rock that bulges into an overhang. Its shadow looms over me, blotting out the blue sky and my view of the climb beyond. I rest my feet on the last substantial hold and survey the scene. Everywhere I look there are grey rock slabs careening into space. "Spectacular" was how those first two climbers described this place. My stomach starts gurgling. Hungry? Nah ... nervous more likely. You remember the Iceman's choice little saying?

*You fall because you're afraid to fall.* So stop yakking and keep climbing.

The groove beneath the overhanging rock flake allows space for my flattened hands and fingers. I slide one hand along, finger muscles flexing. My legs pivot upward, creating pressure against the rock. I pull myself up a few centimetres.

One leg spins free, struggles to regain rock contact. I'm forced to ease back, but there is nowhere to rest. I glance wildly around, searching for a solution — anything. I lose focus. My muscles are crying out. I suck air into my starved lungs. Jerk one hand from the groove and smear it against the textured rock surface below. Desperate move but I get enough leverage to force my leg up. It works. I gain those few, precious centimetres back.

My hands are greasy from the constant smearing action, but I can't reach the chalk bag — not while dangling out here with not even a ledge between me and the faraway ground. My feet and legs are trembling from the strain. Must keep moving. This shaking is spreading like some contagious disease. If I don't make it up and over this time ...

"Uhhh," I hear the groan distantly as if it's emerging from some other body, not my own.

Every muscle is screaming. The groove opens up. Arms take over. My right foot finds some texture in the rock's smoothness. The friction there eases me up. I feel the thrust of the overhang beneath me. I'm left gasping for breath. But I'm over.

"Yes!" Sunshine and blue sky shower over me like an explosion. I blink, then grin and go boulder hopping. After the crux, it all seems like a walk.

A few metres above me lies the rim. It's a golden ribbon, transformed by the sun, luring me on. After all the toe work, I'm feeling flat-footed and clumsy. I stumble over a grass clump, fall onto my face, start laughing hysterically.

As I'm stretched out, face half buried in the grass, a dark blob materializes at the rim and a voice calls, "Jay?"

# Chapter 9

It takes me a minute to realize that it's Katy up there, calling my name. Though I'm lying here, laughing crazily, my mind is still suspended below the overhang. Time has been fast-forwarding. Was it only a few hours ago that I left home? One thing's for sure — I'm on top of the Wall and it feels like the top of the world. I sit up and see the ocean and the islands in the distance, and everywhere else mountains melting into more mountains. I shut my eyes, but I can still see everything. After the adrenaline wears off, I'm feeling great. My mom would say it's the endorphins kicking in.

Eventually I pick myself up and scramble over the final rock step where Katy is waiting, look-ing grim. I'm half wishing the place was empty. Neither of us says anything, but the questions hang like a whiteout between us. I stand beside her and we look over at the ocean. "So how did you find out?"

"Brad phoned me first thing this morning. He was driving back from Whistler and saw someone on the Wall. Figured it had to be you."

"What did he say?"

"Nothing really. Just what I told you."

"Well, how did he sound?"

"You should know. Why keep asking me? You never told me or Brad anything. All you seem to care about is the Wall here."

My mouth opens and shuts like a hooked fish. No sound comes.

"Well?"

"I couldn't tell anyone. If my old man had found out beforehand I wouldn't be sitting here now."

"You could have left me a note."

"Too risky."

"Oh, thanks."

"Katy, please ..." I try pulling her closer, but she pushes me away. I shouldn't have done that. She'll probably hate me worse than ever. Talk about crash-landing back on earth — I feel like a loser.

"What about Brad?" she asks. And before I can reply she says, "I guess you don't care."

"Hold on, Katy. Like I told you before I couldn't risk telling anyone — not Brad, not my folks, not even you."

"Pretty devious, if you ask me."

I give up and stretch out on the sun-warmed

rocks. Behind closed eyes I feel the dancing brilliance of the sun and the soft, mid-morning breeze. I'm somewhere on the Wall again, watching an eagle sailing overhead. Hand over hand I go, faster and faster, until I'm flying too.

Katy is rustling about. Is she going to leave? This moment would be perfect, except for the distance between us. The untouchable Katy, I sigh. In more ways than one. Somewhere on the far-off highway a truck honks. A whistle blows at the mill. Through half-closed eyes I see Katy checking her watch. "I should try and make my afternoon classes. How about you, Jay?"

I shake my head. "Everyone will know where I've been. I'll avoid school until next week."

"It's up to you, Jay. I'm heading down." She pulls my hiking boots from her pack. "I picked these up on my way. Thought you could use them."

"Thanks, Katy. I wasn't looking forward to limping down the trail in my rock shoes. Do you have any water along?"

She pulls a bottle of juice from her pack and hands it over. Watches me down the liquid — every last drop. "You were thirsty!"

"I left my water bottle on the first ledge."

"You did?"

"I know, it was careless. And I'm still thirsty. Let's head down to the creek."

"Fine by me."

Heat waves are shimmering off the bare rock around us. There's not a cloud in the sky as far as you can see. In the distance, the snow-covered peaks of the Coast Mountains look cool and inviting. It's even hotter hop-skipping our way down the backside trail. We swing around big boulders, sometimes skidding on pebbles, until we hear a splashing sound where the water falls into a small pool.

"Swim?" I ask Katy.

"You can't be serious."

"Just joking. It would be a polar bear swim for sure. I might stick a few toes in and test the water."

"I can't stay long. There's school, you know."

"Too bad."

Silence ... except for the sound of water cascading into the pool. We watch a small bird, a dipper, standing on a rock beneath the falling water. He keeps bobbing up and down, occasionally diving off his rock, and swimming underwater to scoop up a bug or some other goody.

Katy laughs. "Cold doesn't seem to matter to him. He just goes about his business all by himself. No fuss, no bother. Different from people."

"That's for sure."

"Half a cheese sandwich, Jay?"

"Thanks, haven't eaten much today." I tuck into the sandwich. Never has food tasted so good, never has the world seemed so great, now that Katy is sounding more friendly. I've actually done it. I have free soloed the Wall and that has never been done before. "You haven't asked me about the climb," I say finally.

"Nope. You know how I feel about solo climbing. It isn't just the safety question — half the fun is going with friends." She sighs. "You made it up safely, that's all I care about."

The no-nonsense Katy talking. No wonder I'm awe-struck. Still, I can't seem to shut up." It was a tough climb. I got gripped by the scenery once. Thinking about you and Brad and everyone helped me refocus."

"Oh? I'm glad to know we're of some use."

Hmm ... harsh words. I don't know what to say, so I let the words roll by. A guy who is struggling up the trail calls out, "How's the water?"

"Freezing!"

Katy checks her watch. "I don't want to be late."

We run down the trail, passing a few more hikers en route, and finally stumble into the parking lot. It's hard to believe I was standing here not so long ago in the early morning darkness. What I've climbed in a couple hours takes most climbers weighed down with gear a whole day. And those first two guys? It was a different climbing scene, way back in the sixties. I have a feeling my world is changing, too.

"Someone is waving to us," Katy says, pointing to a shady corner of the parking lot.

I see a man standing beside his car. The name *Valley Courier,* is splashed across the car door.

"No way."

"What do you mean, Jay?"

"I'm not talking with some dim reporter when I've barely stepped off the Wall."

"Didn't you expect this?"

"Sure, I knew my climb would hit the news. But I need some breathing space, I'm wasted after the climb. Let's go, Katy."

Too late. The guy is hurrying towards us, waving and looking as if he means business.

"Talk to you later, Jay." Katy gives my arm a friendly pat.

"You're not leaving?"

"I'm already late for class."

"Can't you stay for a few minutes? I'm not sure what to tell him. He might mess things up."

She shakes her head. "You're in this alone. It's like free soloing, right? You have to figure things out for yourself."

Her voice sounds clear and cool as an iceberg. And the weird thing is, it scares me more than any pitch on the Wall.

# Chapter 10

"Can I have a word with you?" the figure hurrying towards me calls.

I watch him zeroing in. The guy must be at least thirty, with a stomach that is lurching up and down with every step. I shut my eyes, half hoping he will vanish from my view. No such luck. His heavy breathing barrels into my face.

"Hi, my name's Sid." A chubby hand mops the sweat from his forehead. "I'm a reporter from the Valley Courier."

"I guessed as much." I shake the hand that is pointed towards me like a loaded gun.

"I saw you on the Wall this morning. You can bet my hands were shaking when I realized you were alone and climbing without a rope."

"Free soloing."

"Whatever you want to call it, there's a sensational story here. I'd like to interview you. How be we wander over to my car and have a chat?"

"Could we save it for tomorrow? I'm pretty beat."

"Um ... lots of people saw you climbing and with your cooperation I'd like to out-scoop the big city newspapers."

"You think they would be interested?"

"That's an understatement. Trust me, they will come running."

As we walk towards his car, I feel my heart pounding. I didn't climb the wall to make headlines, but Sid's words grip me. For a moment, I forget my family, forget Brad, forget everything else ... It's exciting, for sure.

"I don't even know your name," Sid says as he opens his car door.

"Jay."

"I didn't expect anyone so young to be climbing alone. Exactly how old are you?"

"Sixteen. I'll be seventeen this August."

"That's young!" He reaches into the back seat where a laptop and some other equipment is stored.

"I'm in high school here," I add. Comments about my age bother me. They always seem a bit condescending, like, what can you expect from a sixteen-year-old?.

Sid eyes the grey Wall looming above the parking lot. "I can't begin to imagine what it's like up there. No rope, all alone, nothing but empty space. Thinking about it makes me feel queasy.

What's the attraction? Why do you do it? Are you ever nervous?"

Whoa! Slow down, I think. We're travelling too fast.

"So why go up there by yourself?"

A part of me is jumping up and down, so fired to talk. And why not talk about it? I'm proud of what I did. I know it was a real feat. Can you imagine the Iceman's face when he reads the newspaper? So here goes. "Because when I'm up there by myself I'm totally free. There is no one telling me what to do or what not to do. It's about as peaceful a place as you can get."

"Peaceful?" Sid interrupts. "When you're hanging by your fingernails, four hundred metres or so off the ground? Most people would say that peaceful is an ... unusual choice of words."

I laugh at his hesitation. "You mean crazy, right?"

"You're the one who said it — not me. But go ahead, tell me why it's so peaceful."

"Look, the game is in my hands when I'm up there. I don't have to worry about anyone on my rope. I'm responsible for me, myself, and I. If I make a dumb move, too bad. I can't blame it on anyone else. It's the same incredible feeling as being alone in the wilderness. But get careless, whack your shin with an axe and it could be game over. So you use your head, see?"

"Hmm... interesting. As I said before it's not most people's idea of peaceful. But go on."

I'm off and away. "You're living in a different world when you are alone up there. Every little crack, every blade of grass or flower comes alive. It's like your vision suddenly explodes."

Sid eyes me, quizzically. "Sounds like some kind of drug experience. You're high, right?"

I look at him, surprised, but it seems like he's joking. He has a dumb grin on his face.

"Would you like some cherry pie I brought from the take out?" he asks suddenly.

"Thanks, haven't had much to eat today."

He watches closely as I wolf down the pie, squash the stray crumbs with one finger and bring them to my mouth.

"Now, let's get down to the details. You're standing at the bottom of the Wall, looking up. How does a sixteen-year-old kid outperform more seasoned climbers and conquer the Wall?"

Uh-oh. Some of his words I do not like, conquer being one. It's a bad luck word. I have not conquered the wall — it's still there, right?

"Go ahead, Jay." He uses my name for the first time. "Trust me, this will be a fantastic story."

I scarcely hear the click of his tape recorder. Like when the lights dim in a theatre, my surroundings fade out. I'm no longer aware of cars driving into the parking lot or doors opening and shutting. What I do hear is my own voice droning on and on. I'm standing at the bottom of the Wall again, no longer the skinny, too tall, too young kid. Sid doesn't interrupt me. You know why?

Because he's got me sitting right here in his chubby, little palm. He's lapping up the story, and so am I.

I hear the click of the tape recorder winding down and Sid's voice. "One more thing, I'd like a photo with the Wall looming in the background. Can you stand over there?"

"I guess so." I feel silly standing in an empty parking lot. Should I grin and point towards the Wall?

Sid scans his camera's screen and smiles. "I've got a few good shots. Do you want to take a look?"

"Leave it as a surprise," I tell him.

"Well, I guess that's enough for today. Can I drop you off somewhere?"

I shake my head. "The walk will do me good." Anything to delay facing the family. They must know by now.

"Watch for the weekend edition of the *Courier*. If I need more information, or if anything further develops from the story, I'll give you a ring."

It's only after Sid's car has gone that I notice a truck parked in the lot — a red, beat-up, pile of metal. Brad's! How long has he been around? From a distance it looks as if nobody is in the cab, but as I draw closer I see a head draped across the steering wheel.

Asleep? No. The head rises up and I find myself staring into Brad's very wide awake eyes. "What are you doing here, Brad?"

"You asking me? I'm the one who should be asking that question. I saw you on the Wall when I was driving back from work."

"I know, Katy told me. Look, I'm sorry ... really. I didn't tell anyone about my climb. If my parents had found out, the whole plan would have died on its feet."

"Sorry, Jay? You let me go yakking on about my plans and you don't mention that you have something up your sleeve. How do you think I feel?"

"Pissed off."

"For sure." Brad gestures after Sid's departing car. "I see you've even got the press lined up."

"No, I did not have the press lined up, as you put it. Sid was waiting for me when I got down. Nothing was planned."

"Except for the climb. Congratulations, Jay, for a perfectly executed plan. And nice to know you and your reporter are on a first name basis already." The sarcasm in his voice hits me like the smell of garlic.

I reach for the truck handle. "Brad, can we talk?"

Brad brings his fist down on the door lock and starts the engine. "I'd love to ask you about the climb, but I haven't got time now."

"Open up, Brad."

"You think we should talk, eh? Well, once upon a time I thought so, too. Friends talk, right? I was having major doubts about my planned jump, and after we last got together I decided to kill it. Was I ever wrong."

"Brad ... be sensible."

"Sensible? Oh sure, Mr. Perfect. Coming from you that's rich." He stares past me for a moment. The truck engine is out of whack and can barely stay idling. "Oh ... and by the way, I will be going ahead with my jump this weekend."

"Brad, turn off the engine. Please."

He leans out the window and brings his face close to mine. "Almost forgot to say thanks for your help. Or in Jay-speak, *thanks for aiding me in the decision-making process*. Have I got you nailed down right?"

"You have it all wrong, Brad."

"Yeah ... and don't lose sleep over not watching my jump. 'Cause it's pretty clear you won't be there. I'll round up a few High-Rise types and maybe your nice reporter friend. Not to worry — I'll manage."

Brad guns the engine and his truck lurches off, swaying crazily from side to side. I'm left with only the exhaust, the far-off explosions as the truck backfires and coasts down the highway, and Brad's parting words. I pound a fist into the empty air. "Idiot ... idiot!" He can't even drive properly. Go ahead Brad, carry out your crazy jump. I'm not your keeper, am I?

Glancing around the parking lot, I realize that everyone has left. My gaze shifts to the Wall, where the sun is reflecting with the intensity of a cut diamond. Heat waves shimmering off it seem to burn my own skin. How could any living thing exist on that face? I grab my pack and head for the highway, at first walking, then racing madly. Anything to escape the steely grey mirror looming overhead.

# Chapter 11

When I reach the highway I slow to a walk. It's three-thirty, a busy time on the road. Cars swish steadily past, usually an annoying sound, but today it helps to drown out my worries. First Brad, and now my family are waiting around the next bend. I'm off the Wall — not out of trouble.

"Hi, got any change?" A panhandler and would-be hitchhiker wheedles some spare change from my pack. I have barely enough left now to buy some juice and a muffin. Still hungry and thirsty.

I veer off the highway and into town, past the high school. From a safe distance I watch Katy playing soccer and I hang around until the practice is finished.

"How did the interview go?" Katy asks when she sees me

"All right, I guess."

"You don't sound very enthusiastic."

"Too many other worries, especially Brad."

"I still can't understand why you went ahead with the climb when you knew the trouble it would cause."

"Look at it this way, how many chances does a person get to do a first? If I'd let it go I might be sorry for the rest of my life."

"It's the solo business ..."

"Katy, there are guys soloing all over the map now — in the Bugaboos, Yosemite, Red Rocks ... there are so many good climbers around, if I hadn't done it, I bet you some rock rat would have come along within the year and climbed the Wall — no rope, no gear."

"And you beat them to it. I know you're that good. Thing is, I'd still like my climbing buddy around."

"Thanks, Katy. I plan to stick around a while longer."

Katy stops by a local sports shop where she has been eying some new hiking boots. I should head home, but I'm visualizing me sitting around the family table. I'll be doing a delicate dance, more fancy footwork than I ever needed on the Wall. I follow Katy inside.

"How's Brad?" Katy asks suddenly. "I met him as he was driving into the parking lot and he looked pretty glum."

"Brad? He wouldn't let me squeeze a word in edgewise, even locked me out of his truck."

"Brad was in bad shape before your climb.

Imagine how he feels now. You never told him your plans. You shut him out of your life."

"Shut him out? Listen Katy, I spent ages looking at the jump he wants to pull off. It's nuts. He's out of bounds."

"Did you tell him so?"

"Yes ... maybe not those exact words."

I hear Katy going on and on. "Brad is balancing on a knife edge, surrounded by a bunch of pros. And you're there too, his best friend."

"What can I do if he slams the truck door in my face?"

"Grab him by the shoulders. Make him listen to you. Watch out for your friend."

And as usual every word Katy says rings as true as a solidly placed piton. We hang around a bit longer, until I have to head home. She gives me a quick hug as I leave. Nice. Unexpected too.

***

While walking back home, I find myself staring up at the Wall. The intense light of midday has faded and will soon give way to evening's fiery red. There's already a pink tinge lighting the rock — yet another of the Wall's shifting moods. I was up there — alone. Guess I'll be reading all about it this weekend. And so will Brad.

"Hello," I call from the doorway. Sounds a bit weak, but how else to announce I'm home.

My sister drifts past me, rolls her eyes and

gives me the thumbs-down. I find my mom and dad huddled in the kitchen, talking. About me? Probably.

"Hello." Sounds worse the second time round. They both straighten up and glare at me.

An hour goes by, actually a few seconds, before the ice dam breaks and the words gush over me.

"First we find your room empty. We suspect the worst when we find your pack and hiking boots gone. Then the calls start — Katy, Friendly what's-his-name, the school principal, your friend Brad, some clueless reporter. That's how we learn what our own son is up to."

The words keep pouring out, mom, dad, dad, mom, until I don't know who is saying what. My sister hovers in the background, keeping quiet.

"Sorry for not telling you," I squeeze in during a lull.

"You need to do considerably better than *sorry*, young man."

Eventually I take refuge in my room, dinner plate in hand, because I can't stomach it at the table, all eyes on me. I'm picking away at my food when a knock comes at the door and the old man marches in. "Listen, there's something I need to tell you. When I realized where you were this morning, I grabbed my binoculars and watched from the highway while you were climbing. Um … Jay? You seemed to be having a problem at one point. I was beside myself. There was absolutely nothing I could do except send up a silent prayer. Your mother was sick with worry. I'm glad she wasn't there."

"Yeah, I know."

"No, you don't know. You haven't the slightest inkling of what it was like down here." There's a long silence and I'm afraid I'm in for more lecturing, but a funny look comes into my dad's eyes. "What was it like standing alone, beneath that giant flake?"

"Awesome."

A smile twitches at my dad's mouth. "Awesome ... yes, I can believe that. It was an amazing feat. Nevertheless, if I catch you soloing again on the Wall before you turn eighteen or you are out of this house, I'll bloody well have something awesome to say." A pat on my shoulder and he's gone. As always, my old man is a puzzle. At least he seems to have forgiven me.

Which is more than I can say for Brad. I've tried phoning him how many times tonight, and always the Iceman answers and always Brad is out or can't come to the phone. I try homework for a while and keep drifting off. I read a book until I fall into a dream-filled sleep.

One dream towards morning grabs me and shakes me so violently I lie awake until it's light outside. It's another one of my Brad dreams. I'm standing on a high pinnacle, balancing precariously. There's scarcely room for me, let alone Brad who is teetering beside me. I'm trying to hold onto him but he keeps swearing and yelling at me. "Let go of me, damn it! Idiot ... let me go!" Finally I become so enraged that I do push him away. He tumbles backwards and catapults down the sheer slope without a sound.

# Chapter 12

First thing I hear is the phone ringing. What now? It's Saturday morning, six-thirty. I stumble from bed and grab it on the second ring, hoping the whole house hasn't been shaken awake. Friendly's voice stuns me. "Brad took off a few minutes ago. I tried to talk him out of his jump. The Iceman and Spider went with him. I'll grab a few things and be at your house — ten minutes."

I phone Katy who is already awake and tell her the news. "Of course I'll come. Pick me up? I'll wait outside our apartment."

My sister pokes her head around the corner as I'm leaving and I whisper to her, "Tell Mom and Dad where I'm going, okay?"

Friendly gears his truck down, slow enough for me to jump in and a few minutes later we swing past Katy's place. Traffic is light this early on a Saturday morning, which is fortunate because

Friendly is bent over the wheel doing some serious driving. I check Katy's and my seatbelts to make sure we are well pinned down. Luckily Friendly's pickup is more reliable than Brad's and will probably make it to Whistler.

"They can't be more than half an hour ahead of us," Friendly says.

I nod glumly, glancing at the speedometer. Friendly is keeping to the speed limit, which you'd better do on this narrow and twisting section of the highway. "How did Brad seem this morning?" I ask

"Hard to say. He wouldn't look at me. Kept talking to the Iceman as if I wasn't in the same room."

"My soloing the Wall came at a harsh time for him."

"Look, you were ready for the Wall — like nobody else. You did what you needed to do. You want to keep festering in the past, Jay-walker?"

"I probably should have told Brad what I was planning." I say this more to Katy than Friendly, but she's staying clear of the conversation.

"Drop it, Jay-walker. We got other worries — like how to stop Brad's jump, then how to dislodge him from the High-Rise. Get him into a better living situation."

As usual Friendly zeroes in on the crux. He stops talking and concentrates on negotiating the hairpin curves that lie ahead. I open the window a crack and suck in the fresh air. Already the air feels warm, which means the snow may not have frozen into a hard base overnight. What will this mean for Brad's jump? I try to focus my thoughts on the mountains floating above the valley mist, but today they look cool and indifferent, and part of a different world.

*Brad ... slow down, we're coming,* I think. My mind ricochets the words around like stones in a rockfall.

Although our eyes don't meet, Katy reaches over and touches my hand. Friendly turns on the radio which helps to scatter the image of Brad rushing towards his fate.

"Where to now?" Friendly asks when we reach the outskirts of town. "This resort is so overgrown I can't find my way around anymore."

"Straight ahead, through the next two traffic lights," I tell him. "Now swing a right and go a couple of blocks until we hit the old chairlift access road."

I see the road directly ahead. Tires have run through the melt water, and the marks are still visible on the road. How recent are they ... five minutes, ten minutes, half an hour? Friendly swerves the truck around the sharp corner and up a hill. Water from the high snow banks is seeping across the road. The tires whip it into spray as Friendly guns the engine. We hit an icy patch and the truck slithers sideways. Friendly wrestles with the steering wheel and we finally top the hill where we find Brad's truck parked.

"Out," Friendly orders.

We pause by Brad's truck where his hiking boots are sitting upright on the hood. Three sets of foot tracks, still clearly visible, lead up the road. So they can't be that far ahead. We take off running. Here and there where the sun has dried the road surface the tracks disappear, but I know where they are leading. If I remember correctly, we have to negotiate the switchback before we get a decent view of the slope. Katy, who is ahead, suddenly swings around. "Jay, hurry!"

Has she seen Brad? I push on. One foot hits a stray patch of ice and I lurch forwards and fall. Fresh tracks are staring me in the face. Where I fell, Brad stopped to attach his skis and climb the bank. Snow scuffed onto the pavement has not yet melted.

For an instant I hesitate before glancing up. My eyes follow Brad's ski tracks that traverse the avalanche debris and head across the steep slope. I see where he did his kick turn, then traversed back, the disjointed tracks along the ridge, until ... "Brad!"

The tracks end where the ridge flattens out. Brad is balanced there alone. His skis are wobbling over the edge, pointing straight down. Has he seen us, or is he blinded by the drop below?

"Oh, no," I groan.

I see the sheer drop, the rocks protruding from the snow here and there, the take-off point above the road cut ... but most of all I see the windswept rock tower on the far side that he has to clear.

"We're too late," Katy whispers.

Brad's skis tip over the edge. He has a few seconds to gather the critical speed needed for the take-off. Is the snow fast enough? I force myself to watch. So far he is doing everything right. Head tucked in, body bent low. But has he enough lift to clear the road and far bank?

"Push it Brad," I hear myself yelling. "You can nail it."

For an instant I believe my own words. He hits the lip above the road where the slope levels off. Airborne now. His lift looks good, body leaning forward, skis pointing in a v-shape, until ... one of them drifts off course. Was it the breeze picking up that did it? Whatever, it puts him off balance, tips his body ever so slightly sideways.

Katy grabs my arm, "Can he do it?"

"Dunno."

I spit out the word as Brad begins his descent. The road cut opens beneath him like the jaws of some beast. But he skims over it and looks set to clear the far side. Wait, one ski clips the tower. The impact tosses him sideways, sends him cartwheeling down the slope. He's gone — out of sight.

"Oh my God, Brad!"

We race up the road, catch sight of the Iceman, Spider, and a third person, who were all watching from below. "Useless," Friendly growls. "They could have stopped him. Who's that other guy?"

Looks like ... yes it is Sid. "Reporter from the

*Valley Courier*," I yell over my shoulder. "Same guy who saw me on the Wall."

"Well, he's got the wrong story today."

When we reach the three who seem frozen to the road, Friendly gears into action. "Who's got a cell phone?" He turns to the Iceman. "Seems like you've done it again."

"Done what?"

"Taken Brad on another dangerous ride. Only not ice this time."

The Iceman shrugs. "He wanted to do this. I just tried to help by coming along. Not my fault if he's incompetent."

Sid, who has been fumbling around in his pack, pulls out a cell phone. "Should I phone 9-1-1?"

"Wait till I have a quick look," I tell him.

Katy and I start kick stepping our way up the embankment tower that Brad was set to conquer. Though we're pushing ourselves, we dread what might lie ahead. We stop on top, scanning the snow below. Halfway down where the slope levels out, we see Brad. One leg still has the ski attached. The other leg is splayed out and no ski to be seen. It's likely hung up somewhere in the trees below.

I gulp in air. "Brad?"

No answer. He doesn't move. "Phone 9-1-1!" I shout to Friendly. "Katy and I will head down to him."

"Roger," Friendly calls up. "We'll stay here and wait for the rescue crew, unless you need help."

"Anyone have an extra jacket, a sweater?"

"Sure." Friendly pulls a sweater from his pack and whips off the Iceman's fleece hat. "You don't need that. Way too warm."

Sid hands over his jacket. "I got enough insulation of my own."

Friendly follows our kick steps up the embankment and hands us the extra clothes. He looks down at Brad and shakes his head. "Nasty, little tower. Not what Brad needed."

"Yeah, probably hooked his ski on the rock sticking out here," I say.

Katy and I stuff the clothes into our packs, then lower ourselves down the bank, facing inwards because it's so steep. Where the slope eases off, we alternately run and glissade, only this isn't play. *What if Brad's paralyzed? What if he's dying?* I don't want to think further.

I lean over Brad and gently wipe the snow from his face. It feels like I'm reaching out from some immense distance. His eyes are closed and there is no sign of life until I detect a thin stream of warmth flowing from his nostrils. Gently I place one hand on his chest. Feel it moving. *Brad, you're alive?*

"We need to step on it, Katy. Brad has been lying here for ten minutes and it'll be at least half an hour before the rescue crew arrives."

"Yeah, I'm worried about hypothermia, too."

"Can you hold him steady while I do a quick body check?"

Katy and I both have our wilderness first aid

tickets, but we're not professionals. Hope the crew gets here soon. I feel my hands shaking as I move them over Brad's head. He's lost his helmet. Did he even have one? I can't remember.

"Still unconscious and probably in shock. An open cut on his head. Not much swelling there yet. And he's breathing all right. That's the big thing." I'm talking half to myself, half to Katy as I check Brad. "Don't like the way his leg is twisted or the way he's lying."

"Can we risk taking his ski off?" Katy asks.

"It'd make it easier for the rescue crew. But in case he has some spinal injury we have to be super careful not to move him."

As I fiddle with the rusty binding that Brad has rigged on his old skis, I shake my head. It looks more like a bear trap than a ski binding. It's a miracle he sailed as high as he did with this contraption.

After we have the ski off, Katy helps me dig a trench under Brad's neck and we stuff Sid's jacket there. I whip off my fleece vest and drape it and Friendly's sweater over his chest. Katy does the same. Not much else we can do except count the minutes until Search and Rescue arrives. I place my hand over Brad's upturned palm. Did I feel a tremor ... "Brad?"

No response.

*Gotta keep you warm, Brad. Can't let you go now.* I squeeze his fingers. Again I sense movement. "Brad?"

Are they ever coming? The sun is flooding the lower slope, but it will be a while before we emerge from the bank's shadow. Funny how old songs spin through your mind when you are stalled in time and waiting. As I watch Katy holding Brad's legs steady I hear myself humming. Don't remember all the words. How does it go? Something about one angel guarding the head, another guarding the feet. Katy is the foot angel. Not sure about me. Our eyes meet and we try a weak smile.

Wait ... I hear something on the road. The high embankment muffles the sound of an engine, doors opening and shutting. A figure appears over the embankment.

I bring my face close to Brad and whisper, "Hang in there, buddy. Won't be long now." His eyelids twitch and a low groan rumbles from his chest. Is he hearing me?

The guy coming towards us turns out to be a woman — young and looking more like a model than a paramedic. Brad would be pleased, if only he knew. After asking us a few questions she turns her attention to Brad. Katy and I shove off, feeling a bit useless.

Within minutes Friendly and two other people appear above us. We watch as they skillfully maneuver a bulky rescue sled down the slope, one guy guiding it at the front, the others gripping the back. "Pretty efficient," Katy says, her eyes focused on the Search and Rescue types.

I have to do something — anything that will take me away from the pale face lying in the snow. My hands won't stop shaking. I start rounding up Brad's stray gear. Both his gloves were ripped off by the impact and are lying on the snow, palms upturned as if they're praying. I shake out the snow and stuff them into my pack. The runaway ski I find lodged deep in a snow hollow carved by wind. While I'm retrieving the ski, the sun floods the lower slope where I'm standing and moves towards Brad. I race the sun up, reaching Brad as the first rays touch his outstretched legs.

"Any news? Is he going to be okay?" I ask Katy who is standing apart from the others.

"Not sure. They've been working on Brad and are pretty tight-lipped."

"Did you overhear anything?"

"Not much. But take a look at this. I found it half buried in the snow."

Katy hands me the battered helmet Brad was wearing. I trace my finger along a crack that has almost split the thing apart. *Brad, how could you? This was ready for the garbage even before your jump.* "You think he has a skull fracture?"

"Could be. I haven't heard them say so."

After turning Brad's helmet over and over in my hands, I have to drop the thing. "Anything else to report, Katy?"

"He could have a broken leg, or a spinal injury. They're being super careful not to move him."

"Wish I could help more."

Katy squeezes my hand. "You were the first to reach Brad and look after him. You found his gear. They will probably want your help pulling the sled up the steep slope. You've done everything you can, Jay."

"I wish." I'm thinking of all the days and weeks before Brad's jump.

We watch as the Search and Rescue crew immobilize Brad — placing straps around his legs, arms, upper body — before transferring him onto the sled. More straps there to pin him down. Block on either side of his head. It's a delicate operation and they do it efficiently. But when I see Brad's face, whiter than the snow around him, I'm scared. More scared than I've ever been climbing some sheer rock face.

Finally, we are on the way. Katy and I follow the crew, until they stop beneath the tower. It's in the shade here and cold — not a good place to hang around. I keep an eye on Brad as they rig up a rope system to secure and pull the sled up the last few metres. Did I see his eyelids flicker? I nudge Katy. "I think he's coming to."

She watches Brad for a moment, shakes her head. "Maybe wishful thinking."

While the sled is being drawn up the embankment, Katy and I kick step our way up on either side, steadying and easing it over one or two protruding rocks. It feels good to be actually helping. My hands and everything else are freezing. Then Friendly is reaching a warm arm down and helping Katy and me over the embankment.

"There's an ambulance waiting further down the road," he tells us. "Why don't you try and go with it, Jay? I'll drive Katy. We'll see you at the hospital."

I chase after the Search and Rescue crew who are really stepping on it. They are dragging the sled along the roadside where there's snow left. This speeds the operation. By the time I catch up they have reached the ambulance. The back door is open and the engine is running.

"Can I ride back here with him?" I ask the ambulance attendant.

She hesitates. "Are you a close friend?"

"Yes."

"I guess it's okay then."

At the last minute, Sid comes struggling up and hands me Brad's wallet, hiking boots and a few other things left in the truck. "I have Brad's keys. We'll drive the truck back. And there's something I want you to know ... when I saw the actual jump he was planning, I tried to stop him. As you've seen, I didn't have any luck."

"Thanks Sid." He's obviously a nice guy, worried about a kid he only just met. Was my first impression of him ever off the mark.

After asking me a few basic questions about Brad, the ambulance attendant focuses on her patient. The questions remind me how little I know about Brad's past. Sure ... during a sleepless night, bivouacking on some cliff face, we talked.

But it was minimal stuff, and I never took the time to dig deeper. "Brad," I whisper. "Give me another chance, okay?"

Once we're on the main road the siren starts wailing and cuts out further talk. I rest my hand on Brad's arm, watching his face. Sometimes pain flashes across it. All the way to the hospital I'm talking, whether he hears me or not. "Hang in there, Brad. We'll be at the hospital soon. The docs will fix you up. I know they can."

I feel his fingers squeeze my hand. His eyes open and he says the word I've been waiting for. "Jay."

# Chapter 13

How to describe the weeks following Brad's accident? It feels like I've been sitting on the back of a speeding motorcycle, heading God knows where. Though I'm clinging to the driver I haven't a clue who or what he is. All I know is, he's a mighty reckless driver and the scenery is out of this world.

I'll start with Brad. After some days in hospital he was transferred to a rehabilitation centre where Friendly, Katy and I have been visiting him. Friendly always brought along some groaner jokes and junk food, which helped cheer Brad up. But two fractured thoracic vertebrae, plus a broken tibia and some smashed ankle bones, is no joke.

Meanwhile, I'm feeling the consequences of my solo climb. My world has shrunk. No visiting the Hilton High-Rise, no rock climbing by myself, no evenings out until I've caught up with my schoolwork, and no skipping school for any reason *whatsoever* — my principal's word. I haven't been sent to a shrink, yet. But if this goes on I may need trauma counselling. My folks say I'm getting off lightly and it's a wonder I haven't been expelled from school. Right on!

Fast forward to the present. I'm standing on top of a pass, staring down a glacier to the lake far below. I lean on my ski poles taking in the scene. It's a stellar spring day — sunshine, corn snow, Coast Mountains to the north and south. What more could anyone want? It's the long-promised ski trip my mom was talking about. The whole family is here, plus Katy who had to do some fancy footwork to join us.

I said it was a perfect day and it is, except for one thing — the family is arguing. Correction, dad and I are discussing just when and where we should rope up. The others are standing around, munching chocolate.

"This is the perfect place to rope up before we step onto the glacier proper," dad is saying.

"It's no treat skiing with a rope," I remind him.

"Better than landing at the bottom of a crevasse. Never go unroped on a glacier — smart little maxim."

I detect the beginning of his famous, upside-down smile. He knows I get riled about stupid little rules. Yes, a rope is sensible, but where the glacier is flat and the crevasses are clearly visible it's overdoing it. "Why not rope up further down where the glacier gets steeper?"

Eventually, Katy and I lead off on the first rope. My mom, sister and dad follow on the second rope, well behind us. This combination bugs my sister. But my mom is not in discussion mode.

"I just want to ski," she says as Katy and I push off.

Even though we're on opposite ends of a rope, it's great to be skiing with Katy. Brad's accident has brought us together like nothing before. "Yee-haw!" we shout, linking telemark turns. Sun overhead and snow flying into our faces as we turn. This is IT.

Katy swings a turn, letting herself slide backward, until the rope jerks her to a stop. I follow her tracks. Below us, where the glacier tumbles towards the lake, the slope gets steeper and there are more crevasses. Above us the snow stretches to the pass, unbroken expect for our ski tracks. The three small dots that are making their way down are still far off. And who cares? My skis slip easily around Katy's as I drift to a halt facing her. She pulls me closer, until our foreheads are touching. "How come?" I start to ask. And then I am holding her and ski-drifting into dreams I don't know where.

"Uh-oh!" Our skis are slipping and we are swaying, collapsing into the snow and laughing hysterically as we struggle to untangle skis and poles and rope.

"So how come, Katy?" I finally manage.

She hesitates, unusual for Katy. "You mean ...?"

"I mean when my climbing buddy morphed from a prickly caterpillar into a butterfly."

Katy makes a face and laughs. "Well, thanks a lot, Jay. Ever think you might have changed, too?"

"Since when?"

"Since Brad's accident."

"In just a few weeks I've changed, Katy?"

"Definitely. In a few days the whole world can change."

"For the better of course."

"Of course." Katy points up the glacier where the three dots are growing into three distinct people. The noise level is also mounting. "They're coming."

"Yes," I say, heaving a sigh, "they are coming." I watch my sister schussing ahead on the rope, almost pulling Mom over. Dad is shouting as he lets out rope, "For heaven's sake slow down or we'll all be ploughing snow." Another interesting day with the family.

"I saw you two hugging," my sister keeps saying. Everyone ignores her.

After sorting out ropes and equipment, we start down the steeper section. Dad leads off with the first rope, Katy and I follow, staying a safe distance back. I keep a watchful eye on the crevasses that spread like thin fingers from the rock walls beside the glacier. Where the crevasses are open, we have to locate a safe bridge or find a way around. Because it's early spring in the mountains many crevasses are still plugged with snow, making it difficult to spot them.

I keep one eye on my old man. Sometimes, after glancing sideways at a crack that seems to have petered out, he stops and sticks his ski pole into the snow, decides it's safe, and pushes on. Trouble is, there's always that slight margin of error in climbing, driving, biking ... whatever. And that's when it happens.

"Aaah!" A sudden yelp from my dad, and he has disappeared.

My sister is jerked forward by the sudden weight on her rope. Mom pulls her rope tight, sits down with her skis edging into the snow, and braces herself as best she can. My sister recovers, drags in the slack rope and also positions herself sideways.

Katy and I push ahead where we see two poles waving from the crevasse. A shaky voice calls out. "Don't worry. I'm not hurt."

"I'll get a belay on his rope just in case," Katy tells me as she drags out her ice axe and plunges it into the snow.

"You do that. I'll go see how he is."

When I peer over the edge I see my dad's face looking up. "Something tells me we should have been belaying one another," he says.

"Aw, Dad, nobody would belay here. It'd take forever. The crevasses are pretty obvious."

"Well this one wasn't, at least not to me."

"We'll have you out in a second."

"Good. Can't say I like being stuck here."

And I can see why. As I look down I see my dad wedged sideways between two ice walls where the crevasse narrows. Below him, the slot widens into a gaping hole, dark except for a few shafts of sunlight striking the blue ice walls. One look into that cavernous hole is enough. I'm thankful Katy has him on belay.

"Can you get your skis off and hand them up?"

"I'll try."

"You got my rope, Katy?" I lie on my stomach, peering over the crevasse edge. With both arms reaching down I can almost touch Dad's head. I hear him groaning as he pulls a ski up and loosens the binding. He hands up one ski, then the other. I place them upside down on the snow so they can't run away.

"How are you doing, Dad?"

"I need a moment to catch my breath before climbing out."

"Would a couple of ascenders help? I even brought the old rope ladder you wanted along."

I hear him laugh. "You did, eh? Well, that's a change."

My shoulders have been feeling the extra weight, what with sleeping bag, first aid kit, emergency locator, food for two days ...

"If you keep the rope tight, I should have enough traction to chimney my way out."

"Not to worry, Dad. We've secured your rope."

I'm not sure he is right about climbing out on his own. The crevasse walls look pretty glassy and vertical to me. Nothing happens for a moment. Wish I could see what's going on, but I've moved back from the edge, tightening his rope. Sudden scratching and some swear words I've never heard from Dad. One hand claws at the crevasse edge. I pull in more slack.

"Give me a minute." he calls up.

I turn to Katy who has my rope. "I think my old man is spent. Let's give him a hand, put him out of his misery."

"Say when you're ready," Katy says.

"Dad, you're almost out. We'll give you a pull." No more arguing. "All right. I'm ready."

A couple minutes later and Dad sits on the snow, looking a bit dazed and rumpled. He shakes himself like a shaggy dog waking from a nap, and after the usual family back and forth — *Thanks everyone. No prob. Should have taken more precautions, I'm the one who is always saying that. No sweat. It was bad luck, nothing more* — we are on our way again.

Once off the glacier we unrope and ski full out. As dad would say *we hoot and holler it* all the way down to the cabin where we're spending the night. The snow is great, the sun is great, Katy is great and the family isn't half bad either. I'm one lucky guy. Can't help thinking about Brad and wondering how he is doing at this exact moment.

\*\*\*

Later, after polishing off a spaghetti dinner, we sit around the stove and talk. Dad keeps rehashing the crevasse affair until Mom calls a halt and says, "I'm turning in."

I lie awake on my bunk listening to the usual cabin sounds — the occasional pop as the stove contracts, a pack rat gnawing something, snuffling from my dad's corner, the steady breathing from the bunk overhead where Katy is sleeping.

Water drips from the cabin roof, a loose ice chunk rattles down the cedar shakes, the stream where we fetch water collapses a snow bank and carves out another cave, an owl hoots. Though I can't hear it, I know that somewhere down where blue ice forms, the glacier is shifting and ever-changing.

# Epilogue

Epilogue, conclusion, postscript, or as Sid would say, we're going to polish off the story. That's because later today Brad and I are meeting him for the last time. This latest interview will wrap up his series on extreme sports. He's talked to Friendly, the Iceman and Spider. By now he has a good feel for what is a reasonable risk and what's out of bounds. Talking to Sid has been good for Brad and me. Maybe we're not the same two guys, but we're the same old friends.

At the moment Katy, Brad, Friendly and I are wandering towards the Bluffs. I say wandering because Brad is still shaky on his feet, six months after the accident. He is walking with a cane. "I gotta sniff some climbing air," he keeps saying.

"Whew!" Friendly points to the rock shoes slung around Brad's neck. "They smell rank enough. What else do you want?"

"You'll see. There was a story in the paper about some guy who lost his foot in a car accident. They fitted him with this metal thing where his foot used to be. Now he's back to climbing. If he can do it, why not me?"

We stop beneath Beginner's Burp, the easiest route around, and junk our gear. Friendly brought along a breakfast picnic as he calls it. "It'll cheer Brad," he told me. "If the climbing doesn't pan out, at least there'll be food."

He drags a dish towel from his pack and spreads it on the ground. Pours granola into four plastic bowls, slices up some bananas and apples, and tops the whole works with yogurt. "Voilà," he says, handing Brad a spoon. "Today you eat healthy."

"Wow, man. I didn't know you were a chef. After snow boarding you've got a whole new career coming up."

This is sounding like my old climbing buddy. During that first week at the rehabilitation centre Brad sank to rock bottom. "Why bother?" he spat out more than once. "I'll never climb again. I'll be lucky to walk on level ground again. The docs have said it. I know it, you know it, everybody knows it. So why fool around?"

It took all my willpower to travel down to the rehab centre and face Brad and the wall he had put up. It was higher than any wall I had ever scaled.

"We'll drive down together," Friendly kept insisting. Together we told Brad to get off his butt, though not in those words. And an older patient, a guy who had almost died in a fall, really helped. Day after day, Brad watched him struggling with the exercises, and gradually his determination and optimism rubbed off on Brad.

"More granola anyone?" Friendly asks. "Otherwise I'll pack everything away."

"You climbing first, Brad?" I ask.

He scans the rock face, hesitates for a moment, "Sure, I'll have a go."

Friendly stays below to help Brad while Katy and I scamper up the rock. Even Katy goes ropeless here. After setting up Brad's belay we relax and wait for the signal that he's climbing. No hurry down there. And take your time, old sun. Go dance on the ocean. It's morning and Katy and I have all the time in the world.

"Would you do the climb again?" Katy asks pointing towards the Wall

"By myself? Sometime maybe. But I'm in no rush. It won't run away."

"Your parents might want a say. And don't forget about me."

"Yes, and that too." I try out my dad's perfect, upside-down smile.

"You look just like your dad."

"Oh no."

I feel a tug on Brad's rope. "Ready to climb," he calls.

I watch Friendly cup his hands and give Brad a hoist so he can reach the first big step. I keep the rope tight, telling him to arm-wrestle his way up if the footwork gets too painful. Slow going, but he does it. He's at the top, grinning until I swear his teeth are curling.

"Way to go, Brad."

"Thanks, Jay. I got nothing but chicken legs here." He taps his wasted muscles.

"Give it time."

"Sure. Good thing the ski season is a few weeks off. It'll be a while before I can start teaching kid's ski classes."

We watch Friendly barrelling up the rock. "Nice," he says, sitting down beside us and clapping Brad's shoulder.

After we've been watching the scenery for a while I check my watch. "Brad, in half an hour we're meeting Sid. Remember?"

I start down the steep trail first, Brad gripping my shoulders for support. Friendly stays behind, holding a sling tied around Brad's waist. "You look like a runaway toddler, Brad."

"You think I don't feel like one?"

When we reach Sid's office Katy and Friendly take off.

"See you two for dinner tonight at our place," I call after them. I say *our place*, because Brad is living with my family until he gets back on his feet. It seems Dad doesn't mind Friendly, either. They can sit around arguing until it drives everyone else insane. Great minds think alike, I guess!

I stare at the Wall gleaming in the afternoon sun. As I've said before, it dominates our town's scenery, but in my own mind it has shrunk to a workable size. Everything in perspective, I think.

"It was good, eh?" Brad has been watching me.

"It was."

"I can imagine. I'll never get to go there, not how you did."

"Look, Brad." I'm pointing north, south, east ... where the mountains stretch to the horizon. "There's lots waiting for you and me out there. And if you decide to go west, we can kayak all the way to Japan. "

"Right on, Jay." And together we go to meet Sid.

# Fifty Years Out
## Physicians Reflect on Our Times

A collection of essays contributed by members of
the Harvard Medical School Class of 1953

Editors:
Fritz Loewenstein
A. Scott Earle
Donald N. Wysham

HOLLIS
PUBLISHING

ISBN-10: 1-884186-35-1
ISBN-13: 978-1-884186-35-6

Printed in the United States of America

Hollis Publishing Company
95 Runnells Bridge Road, Hollis, NH 03049
(t) 603-889-4500  (f) 603-889-6551
books@hollispublishing.com